Also By Steven Becker

Kurt Hunter Mysteries
Backwater Bay
Backwater Channel
Backwater Cove
Backwater Key
Backwater Pass
Backwater Tide (Sept 2018)

Mac Travis Adventures
Wood's Relic
Wood's Reef
Wood's Wall
Wood's Wreck
Wood's Harbor
Wood's Reach
Wood's Revenge
Wood's Betrayal

Tides of Fortune
Pirate
The Wreck of the Ten Sail
Haitian Gold

Will Service Adventure Thrillers
Bonefish Blues
Tuna Tango
Dorado Duet

Storm Series
Storm Rising
Storm Force

ISBN: 978-1732596009

A KURT HUNTER MYSTERY

BACKWATER PASS

LARGE PRINT

STEVEN BECKER

In March of this year (2018), the FIU walking bridge, built using a new type of engineering called Accelerated Bridge Construction, collapsed on Highway 41 and killed six people. The investigation is ongoing as are the lawsuits and talk of criminal indictments. Now, almost six months later, there are as many conspiracy theories as facts. Backwater Pass is my own spin on what could have happened. The book is purely a work of fiction. Though the collapse is accurate, my portrayal is not meant to reflect on any person or company involved in the design, construction, or investigation. I would like to extend my deepest condolences to the victims and families.

Steven Becker - July 2018

Chapter 1

The bones of the old boat were calling us through the thirty feet of crystal clear water. Allie, Justine, and I leaned over the side of the boat staring down at the wreck. Shipwrecks have a certain romance to them and this one, although not an eighteenth-century Spanish galleon, was every bit as compelling. Our minds wandered back in time to New Year's 1966 when the ill-fated luxury yacht, running twenty miles off course in ten-foot seas, embedded itself in the reef. All aboard had been lifted by Coast Guard helicopters and taken ashore. There had been no casualties, except whatever remained below the glimmering surface.

Allie, Justine, and I had spent the last few weekends scouting for lobster season and enjoying a part of the Biscayne National Park that I wasn't all that familiar with. Most of my year as a special agent here had been spent on the inside of the barrier islands. That was where most of the action that concerned me took place. Lying within a stone's throw of Miami, for centuries the miles of undeveloped coastline and mangrove-lined channels had been a smugglers' haven. And since the boundary between the park and state waters was only a dotted line on a chart, the Coast Guard and ICE handled most of the offshore action. There was plenty for me on the inside. Since being stationed here as part of what I like to call the "witness protection program of the National Park Service", I had found my share of contraband, as well as several floaters.

I had learned the inside waters of the park by fishing, an activity that as often as it landed its intended target also found trouble. Fishing was a way for me to enter a kind of flow state where I could see things differently. Maybe it was the primitive brainwave signal when we turned from prey to predator or just the anticipation that anything could happen at any time, but I did my best thinking with a rod in my hand. When it had come time to choose where I was going to transfer, the water here had played a large part in my decision.

My daughter Allie had been recently certified as a diver and I was still a novice, leaving us to rely on Justine, my girlfriend, for instruction. Lobster were protected inside the park, pushing us outside of the park boundary where we had spent the day scouting groups of coral heads and shallow reefs in anticipation of the Sportsman's mini season. Throughout the state, the last weekend of July was reserved for recreational divers to take lobster before the commercial traps were set. There was no guarantee the crustaceans would be there next weekend, but if they were, scoping things out early would give us an advantage.

My GPS was loaded with locations—more spots than we could check in the two days of the mini-season—so we decided to check out some of the wrecks inside the park.

"Hey, Dad, which one is this?"

"I think it's the *Mandalay*. The *Laguna* is to the north." With the semi-waterproof chart from the gift shop spread out on top of the console of the boat, I traced the Maritime Heritage Trail with my finger and confirmed my guess.

"How much air do you guys have?" I asked.

They went to their gear and checked the gauges.

"Twelve hundred," Allie called out proudly.

"Almost two thousand," Justine said. "What about you?"

I hesitated, not wanting to be the low man, but diving is a sport where you have to put aside your ego. "Just over a thousand." Justine's experience accounted for her minimal air consumption and Allie was a natural. I sucked air like a pig. "It'll give us a good twenty minutes," I said, roughly calculating my own consumption at the shallow depth. This was the end of our second tanks, and after multiple drops on different areas, I had gotten a feel for how quickly I burned through my air supply."

"Let's stay together and make sure the boat is in sight when Pops here has five hundred left." Justine gave me a look that told me I would be in big trouble if I didn't comply.

Several minutes later we were geared up and one by one we rolled over the side of my park service's twenty-two-foot center console—one of the perks of the job. The water was so clear that when I looked up, I was worried about hitting my head on one of the old beams that had made up the hull of the ship, but I found my equilibrium and finned to the mooring line. I looked around for Justine and Allie, who were twenty feet away and already exploring the wreck. Out of habit, I glanced at the surface and relaxed when I saw ours and the other five white balls allocated for the wreck and hoped that not having to worry about the anchor pulling would help with my air consumption. After I finned toward them we grouped up and gave each other the "okay" sign.

The bottom came up quickly and I pressed the inflator button to attain neutral buoyancy and not smash one of my body parts into a piece of the fifty-year-old wreck. I had been reluctant to dive on something so new, thinking the older bones of a Spanish Galleon would be more exciting, but seeing the intact framework for the ship covered with multi-colored marine growth was fascinating. The saltwater and currents had long ago eaten away the wooden hulls of the older boats, often leaving little more than a pile of ballast stones to mark their graves. But as we swam around the hundred-plus-foot hull of what had once been a state-of-the-art luxury yacht, I could almost envision the New Year's party on her last night at sea.

We had intentionally stayed shallower than

thirty-three feet all day, so there were no calculations or worries about decompression sickness. Air was our limiting factor diving this shallow, and when I looked at my gauge and saw the needle deep into the red area that showed I had less than five hundred psi left, I reached for a brass clip I had on my vest, removed it, and reaching behind me banged the tank with it.

Within seconds Justine and Allie were by my side, and we swam together toward the bow of the wreck where the mooring line was secured to a huge concrete block. Surprisingly I had a few hundred more psi than Allie, who still wanted to push the limits and continue the dive. Justine had decided that the only way Allie would learn to respect the privilege of breathing bottled air was to run out. We continued and a few minutes later I was alarmed when I saw Allie take that last breath: I don't think I'll soon forget the panicked look on her face when she realized her tank was empty. Justine was right there with her octopus, a secondary regulator for just this purpose, and handed it to her. Allie's training took over and the two buddy-breathed to the surface. I promised myself to thank Justine later for the lesson.

The swim ladder was only a few feet away when it was my turn to experience the pull of nothing as I tried to inhale and felt only resistance in return. My father had taught me the rules to being a gentleman, and I generally followed them, but not this time. I kicked hard for the ladder and was first aboard.

After dropping my tank and BC on the deck, I helped Allie and Justine aboard—but not before kicking my air gauge under my gear to avoid the certain lecture I would get if either of them saw the needle bottomed out. Twenty-two feet of boat is not a lot of room for three divers' gear so we stripped our tanks and stowed our fins, BCs, and regulators in the console before dropping the mooring buoy and heading back to Adams Key.

Located just inside of Caesar Creek, the small

island was my home. I shared it with Ray, the maintenance guru for the outer islands, and his family. Zero, the island alarm skidded to a stop on the concrete dock when we pulled up. He barked twice until realizing his two favorite people were aboard, then started groaning softly. Allie, with the bowline in her hand, jumped up to the dock and tied the line off. Zero sidled up to her, pinning her against the piling and demanding the attention he had convinced himself he was entitled to. He had a moment of indecision when Justine hopped up with the stern line, but Allie was working hard to please him. We were usually buddies, but today I was on the bottom of the list and was able to lift our gear onto the dock and hose down the boat while Justine and Allie took turns playing with him.

This was always a hard part of our time together. Allie and I had regained our closeness over the last few months with a big helping hand from Justine. It had been a good time for all of us, and I looked at

Justine as she hosed down our gear, wondering when I would get the nerve to tell her I loved her. Allie was ready for us to get married, but I was a little behind the curve.

The last six months had been some of the happiest of my life, but there had been a hard year leading up to it. I would never forget the small courtroom in Plumas County where Jane, my ex, had taken Allie from me. I had missed a year of her almost sixteen-year-old life, even though I could understand Jane's response: our house had been firebombed by an angry cartel after I had discovered what was, at the time, the largest pot grow on public land. I might still hold the record for that discovery, but following those kinds of stats held little interest for me.

Becky came over with Jamie, her three-year-old, following close behind. "Y'all catch anything?"

"No, just doing some scouting," I said.

"Ought to talk to Ray. He knows where those

buggers are."

"Yeah," I said, and turned to find myself eye to eye with Zero. Allie and Justine had abandoned him to play with Jamie. *Now* I was good enough.

"Y'all want to come up for some snapper? Ray's got the grill going. Caught a bucket full of nice yellowtails this morning."

"Can we, Dad?" Allie asked.

Zero answered the question by barking several times. "Sure." It settled that uneasy time trying to decide how to end the day and take Allie back to her mother. "But, we have to go right after dinner."

"I know."

The typical teenage acknowledgment was given. We brought the dive gear up to the house to dry and headed across the lawn to Ray and Becky's house.

The island had a large clearing that incorporated our two stilt houses as well as a small day-use area. The well-manicured lawn was an unusual feature for the barrier islands, which were typically little more than salt marshes covered with mangroves. Adams Key, formerly called Cocolobo Key, and the adjacent area known as Islandia, had a colorful history. Back in the 1920s speculators had taken what was essentially free land and tried to tame it. Adams Key was one of the few projects that had not been abandoned and it had housed the Cocolobo club, a resort reputed to have been visited by four presidents.

The islands fell into disrepair over the years and after the eye of hurricane Andrew plowed through here in 1992 there was little left to show for the early developers' efforts except for some deep water channels that dead-ended for no apparent reason, and clearings such as this one. Most everything else had been reclaimed by the harsh environment.

The smell of the barbecue sauce and butter mixture Becky used to baste the fish had my mouth watering, and the cold beers sitting in a bucket of ice looked inviting. I was taking Allie home, though, so I stuck with my bottle of water. We sat around the standard-issue park service fire pit. There were thousands just like it in every campground in America, but Ray had customized his. Instead of a partial grill that was rarely clean enough to use, rods welded to the side of the steel ring supported a full-size stainless steel grill that could be set at several heights.

Allie gave Ray a rundown of where we had dived today and I knew she wanted him to offer up some of his super secret spots, but he remained silent, only nodding to her. I knew they supplemented their income by selling lobster and had expected the silence. It was like asking Chico, one of the fishing guides here, for some of his spots—something you just didn't do. The truth was that we'd had a great day of prospecting ourselves. I turned to the fire and watched as the delicious marinade dripped fat onto the coals, creating flames that kissed the underside of the fish.

Several minutes later, the food was ready and we sat down to eat. The same conversation was playing out here as at thousands of other barbecues in Florida: where to find the lobster this coming weekend.

Eventually, we finished dinner and said our good-byes. Zero followed us to the boat and barked as Allie and Justine released the lines and I turned the bow toward reality. Heading into the sunset, I wished I could extend the day, but also knew there would be more to come.

"Wanna drive?" I asked Allie. At six months past her fifteenth birthday she had just gotten her learner's permit. I wasn't ready for her to drive in Miami traffic, but she was confident with the boat.

"Really?"

I moved over and let her take the wheel. She was a little hesitant, causing the ride to be somewhat jerky at first, but the boat came up on plane and I could see the thrill in her eyes as she steered toward the markers leading up to Bayfront Park and the park service headquarters building.

Chapter 2

Divorce with children is complicated and rule number one is to not let your ex-wife near your current girlfriend. Justine continued to amaze me and made every effort to make things work with Jane. They got along, which I considered a stroke of luck, though sometimes it was unsettling when they ganged up against me.

There wasn't the typical animosity between Jane and I that many divorced couples had. Neither of the usual culprits: sex or money, were responsible for our breakup. We already had been heading down the wrong path before the incident. Living in a small town had been a dream for each of us, with the difference being the definition of "small". I was fine with the four-figure number on the sign when you entered the town; she would have preferred another zero on the end. Then our downfall was set into freefall when our home was firebombed by the cartel. I didn't blame her for her reaction.

Though they got along and it was often more convenient for Justine, who lived in Miami, to run Allie to her mom, I preferred to pick up and drop off my daughter whenever possible.

Living on an island had its perks, but any kind of rendezvous needed to be thoroughly planned. Adams Key lay seven miles from park headquarters, where my truck was parked, and it could take anywhere from twenty minutes to an hour to reach it. The weather played as much a part in the time it took to cross the bay as the traffic did on the mainland.

The afternoon sea breeze had kicked up and I estimated that the first part of today's commute would be about forty minutes. It was a little less than that when we pulled into the slip at the small marina beside the headquarters building. This late on a Sunday, the usual suspects were all there: Pete

Robinson's FWC boat, Johnny Wells thirty-nine-foot quad-powered ICE Interceptor, and my counterpart Susan McLeash's matching center console. Allie brushed off my attempt for help and backed into the slip without incident. We secured the lines and headed for the next stage of our journey: Miami traffic.

I gave Allie the *maybe next time* line when she asked if she could drive on land as well, and hopped behind the wheel of the park service pickup. Justine gracefully got in back and Allie jumped in the passenger seat. After starting the truck, I glanced over to make sure her seatbelt was fastened and found her nose buried in her phone. Justine had speculated that Allie had a boyfriend, but I wasn't ready to ask that question yet. Sometimes it's better for a father to be in the dark.

I pulled out of the lot and headed west toward the Turnpike. With one eye ahead and the other on my phone, I started to enter the address of our meeting place into the maps app when Allie grabbed the phone from me.

"Dad," she scolded me.

I ignored the throat clearing in the back seat and relented. The road was dead straight and I was an accomplished knee driver, but now that Allie had her permit, I realized everything I did behind the wheel would be scrutinized.

"Looks like there's traffic on the Turnpike around 836."

"Alternate route?" With the crapshoot that was Miami traffic, using the map app had proven to be a reliable time saver. The technology had advanced to the point that it displayed real-time traffic in either green, yellow, or red. Miami all too frequently was full of yellow lines and red dashes.

"Take the Shula Expressway to the Palmetto and get off on 41. That should take us around it."

It bothered me that map reading was becoming a lost art, but this was still cool. I followed her directions and a half hour later exited the Palmetto and took a left onto 41, which would take us back to the Turnpike.

"You thought any more about what colleges you want to look at?" I asked after seeing the sign for Florida International University.

"Gators, if they'll take me."

I breathed a sigh of relief at the prospect of having to pay in-state tuition. I was about to ask if she had a backup plan when I heard a loud crash and brake lights flashed ahead of us. Suddenly the traffic came to a standstill and a cloud of dust rose from the road ahead. I didn't have to look at Justine to know this was worse than a fender bender. I slammed on the brakes, barely missing the car in front of me, and set the lever to park. "Allie, stay here," I said and got out. Justine was next to me.

"This looks bad. I'll call 911 and Miami-Dade," she said.

We took off at a run. People were out of their

cars now, looking for the cause of the backup. After running another block, I saw what looked like a wall blocking the road. Justine and I were both trained as first responders and didn't hesitate. It became evident after another hundred feet what had happened and I steeled myself for what lay ahead.

The pedestrian walkway across the highway had collapsed. Huge concrete pieces lay askew and several had fallen directly on vehicles. There was a general sense of panic surrounding the scene, which only increased when we heard the first sirens. Miami-Dade would be here momentarily; the important thing for us was to find the victims.

Justine and I ran over to the first car and saw that a concrete beam had completely crushed the driver. There were two people in the backseat holding each other and crying. Justine went to them and I moved to the next vehicle. Over the next half hour I did what I could, until Miami-Dade took over and Justine and I were eased out of the way. With our heads down we walked back to the truck.

Allie had her head down and I assumed she was texting her boyfriend when we got back.

"Is it as bad as it looks?" she asked. She held up a YouTube video of the collapse that had already been posted.

Covered in dirt and grime, we looked at each other. "Yeah." It didn't escape me that if we'd been here two minutes earlier we could have been under that debris. "It's bad. Can you call your mom?"

"Already did. She's cool, just said to text her when we can get out of here."

Trying to force the images I had just seen from my head, I surveyed the scene. The sun had set and in place of another famous Florida sunset was a display of red, white, blue, yellow, and green lights from the emergency vehicles. Several police cruisers were behind us directing traffic to allow the trapped vehicles an exit route. There was nothing else to be done here, and after getting back in the truck, I followed the directions of an officer with an orange vest and flashlights in each hand. He directed me to turn around by pointing one light toward a side street.

"You guys okay?" I knew I wasn't, but one of the first duties of the living was to keep moving. They both responded quietly and I followed the road north past several golf course communities until reaching the Turnpike at the next exit.

"Did people die?" Allie asked.

"I think so." I wanted to say something to comfort her, but the words would not form sentences.

"It's a terrible accident. The police and firefighters will do everything they can," Justine said.

I looked over at Allie. She had started to look older and more mature to me, but now she looked like the younger version I remembered after our house had been destroyed. I reached over to take her hand and she grasped mine hard. We didn't let go until we pulled into the designated parking lot a half hour later to meet Jane.

Allie ran to her and they embraced. It hurt a little to watch, but I knew the two had gone through a lot together and had a strong bond. Jane had actually showed some wisdom when she had decided not to resist my attempt for some time with Allie, telling me that if she kept us apart she would be driving Allie away from her in the process.

"Looked pretty bad on the Internet," she said.

"Yeah." I realized how I must look. "Allie waited in the truck while we checked out the scene before the paramedics arrived." Allie and I had a long hard embrace and I wiped the tears from her eyes before saying good-bye. Justine held her close for a long time as well. Jane indulged us and we finally left to our separate Monday-to-Friday routines.

"What do you want to do?" Justine asked.

We had originally planned on spending the night at her apartment. I could think of nowhere else I would rather be, but something was bothering me. “Can we go back to the scene?”

“I’ll bite. I have to admit I’m curious as well.”

Justine worked the swing shift at the forensics lab. She’d seen death and destruction in a myriad of settings. We had both gotten over being close enough to the accident to be aware that if it had happened a few seconds later, we would have been underneath it. Now our clinical brains were taking over and I was curious. Highway 41 was a major east–west road and the debris would be cleared quickly. If we wanted to see what had happened this might be our only chance.

We came in from the west on 41, figuring it would be an easier escape route. Apparently we weren’t the only ones with this idea. Justine’s credentials got us through the checkpoint setup to divert traffic at the Turnpike, but we ground to a stop a hundred feet later. The road was clogged with what looked like every vehicle Miami-Dade had, scattered randomly wherever they had stopped. We parked off to the side and I grabbed my credentials from the glove compartment. I wasn't sure where they would get me, but they looked official.

I recognized several faces as we approached the collapsed bridge, and Justine said muted hellos to others. Generators hummed, powering the large construction lights that had been brought in, and people in and out of uniform, each looking like they knew what they were doing, worked the scene. With no assignment, we stood and stared at the rubble like tourists.

The site was so busy that no one bothered to question us as we walked around. Justine started taking pictures of the broken sections with her phone. I thought about doing the same except Martinez, my boss, would want to know why I was here. As special agent in charge, he did his job from behind his desk, watching his three large-screen monitors, which showed him more of my life than I wanted him to know. I had learned the hard way that everything I did, and everywhere I went, was monitored. The boat, truck, and phone were all park service issue. He knew my location at all times and all the data on my phone went to the Cloud where he could see it.

Still, it was a unique perspective to be looking at the wreckage from a ten-thousand foot view instead of focusing on a small part of it like investigators were prone to do. The park service has been my career for almost a decade, but before that I was in construction. I had worked for my dad on a framing and concrete crew in high school and returned to work full-time in his employ after a brief stint in college.

I had read about this project. Using accelerated bridge construction or ABC, the bridge was built to be assembled in sections, then cranes would swing them into place so as to avoid closing the busy road. The standard procedure, for as long as anyone had been building bridges, had always been to shut down one side of the highway while that section was being built, then move to the other side to complete the structure. On a highway that saw as much traffic as this, that would only add to the nightmare of driving in Dade County. ABC would put the bridge in place in a weekend.

Looking around I studied the scene. Rebar, the steel that gave reinforced concrete its strength, stuck out of some of the broken pieces that still stood on each side. These were the sections that were built traditionally, as they were out of the traffic pattern. It looked like those had crumbled after the initial failure. In the center of the road, the pre-cast finished sections lay in a jumble, but seemed to be mostly intact. We wandered over to one of them. Concrete by itself is a brittle material. It needs the steel reinforcing bars embedded inside it for strength. If the bridge had been built in place, there would have been a maze of reinforcing bars running through the concrete; instead there were only several large tensioning rods.

“Looks like it failed here,” I said.

Chapter 3

After a restless night, I sat at Justine's table drinking coffee, glued to the non-stop news coverage of the bridge collapse, and wondering why Martinez hadn't called. I had no doubt he knew where I was from the location of the truck and the phone. Generally, when I stayed here, he was my alarm.

Justine was out training for a paddleboard race she had coming up. Lately, I'd been going out with her on her long slow days, which for me were long fast days. She was good about circling back for me and I felt like I was getting better. My assignment here at the park was less strenuous than walking miles in the forest every day. Living on an island and having a boat at my disposal for transportation had put a few extra pounds around my midsection.

Looking at forty I knew that wasn't a good thing, but recently I had started to do a body weight training program and hoped that between that and paddling with Justine I could reverse that course.

Justine was still out when I finished my coffee. The news had become redundant and I decided to head back down to the park. It was too early in the investigation to reveal anything useful and the talking heads were just speculating. The initial press conferences were over and the clean-up had already begun. I rinsed out my cup and cleaned the coffee pot, then gathered my dirty laundry from my dresser drawer and headed out to the truck.

The after-rush hour traffic was moving steadily, giving me time to think. The last few weeks had been slow, but I knew what we were in for with the coming assault of boaters for Sportsman's weekend. Even though the park was a part of the Biscayne Bay–Card Sound Lobster Sanctuary, many of the hunters passed through its waters. Generally, I split the inside waters of the park into four quadrants and patrolled one a day. That left a day for the paperwork required by Martinez. Today, I thought I might change it up and work north, on the outside of the islands from Elliot Key up to Boca Chita. Tomorrow, I would reverse course and head south.

I wanted to get a feel for some of the small inlets and creeks on the ocean side. Checking licenses and catches was typically under the jurisdiction of the Florida Fish and Wildlife Commission, but the tidal creeks, especially the ones with any kind of structure, were loaded with what some of the locals call "bugs", and I suspected there would be more than a few boaters unable to avoid the temptation of the creeks and canals that wove like a maze through some of the outer keys.

I reached headquarters and saw Martinez and Susan McLeash's trucks parked side by side. Susan was my equal as well as my nemesis. I still hadn't figured out if it was her lack of judgment or her cavalier attitude that usually got her in trouble. Unless her violations were flagrant, Martinez would cover for her, but many were witnessed by outsiders and she was constantly skirting the line between active duty, suspension, or reassignment. The last time she had gone off the reservation it had worked for her, so she had recently been given a commendation and had been reinstated. I guessed there was some probation involved with some of her earlier decisions that she had been sidelined for. But now she was back, and with no call yet from Martinez I was getting paranoid.

Looking up at the security camera by the entrance I walked in the door. Mariposa greeted me with a big smile from behind the reception desk. The matronly Jamaican was my one ally here, as well as a friend.

"So, when do we get to meet your daughter?" Mariposa asked.

I motioned with my head to Martinez's upstairs

office as I approached her desk, thinking he had microphones and could hear our conversation.

"He's been up there for the last two hours meeting with your girlfriend. Came down and asked for a map of the park a little bit ago. It was my pleasure to inform him that we called them 'charts' here."

"What's he up to?"

"Got a call this morning from the chancellor of that University where the bridge collapsed. Now, about your daughter—or do I have to go over your head and call Justine?"

"She'll be down next weekend. How about if we come by Saturday night? You're welcome to come out to the island, too. Hopefully we'll have some lobster."

"You can just come by the house; my husband doesn't like to travel with the Appleton. You bring the lobster and I'll cook them up."

"Deal." Despite the boat ride back and forth, the

dinner would be spectacular and I longed for another taste of her husband's guest-only rum. "I better go see what those two are up to."

I headed upstairs, surprised to see that both Susan and Martinez's offices were empty. Peeking in I noticed his monitors were in standby mode. Down the hall was my office, which was of course empty, and a conference room just past it. The door to the conference room was open and I looked in to see the two of them leaning over the large table, examining what I guessed was the chart Mariposa had mentioned. They were close. Closer than I would have been to either of them.

I cleared my throat. "I was planning on heading out to check the out islands north of Caesar's Creek." I heard only a muffled "okay" in response. Something about the two of them in cahoots had me on full alert. Whatever they were up to could not be good for the park—or me.

Over the last year and a half I had developed a

deep feeling of respect for the ecosystem in our charge. Billed as ninety-five percent water, the park was a unique environment in itself, but its proximity to Miami made it accessible. That was both a blessing and a curse. The more people that visited and experienced the raw beauty of the water and the mangrove-lined shores the more it would be appreciated. On the flip side, the more visitors the park had, the greater the incidence of damage to the fragile environment. Propellers that tore through shallow flats and destroyed the seagrass were the biggest problem, but there were many others.

I decided to stop by my office and kill some time, hoping they would take a break and I could get a look at that chart. Opening the door, I sat in the windowless room and started the computer. Wondering what Martinez would think, I started doing the unthinkable and pecked out a schedule for the week. He insisted on them, but I rarely complied, and often when I did they were written on bar napkins or consisted of one-line emails. Having already laid out the week in my head, it flowed through my fingers and onto the computer screen. I was ready to email it before they left the room.

I thought if I stayed any longer he might get suspicious, so I emailed the attachment and left. Thinking two steps ahead but not paying attention, I bumped into him.

Martinez looked up at me like I was breaking some unwritten rule by being here. "Hunter, I need to talk to you," he said.

Susan brushed by with a smile on her face and I steeled myself for whatever she had set me up for this time. "I just emailed you my schedule."

"My office," he demanded.

I followed him into his lair. As if they knew their master was present the flat screen monitors came to life. He sat down and motioned me to the other chair. It was his habit to make me wait, either through some feigned urgent phone call or email, and this time was no different. I fidgeted in the chair while he read something on his screen. He hit several keys and turned to the bank of monitors.

"You have an explanation for this?"

I stared at the pictures that Susan McLeash had taken of me icing down a pair of mangrove snapper. I knew she had them and wondered why she had chosen now to use them. "That was a while ago," I said.

He ignored me. "Timestamp shows that you were on duty that day. We've been through this about you fishing on duty before. I'm going to have to write you up for disciplinary action this time."

It was actually the first time he had proof. I sat there defenseless, not wanting to give the impression that I didn't care. "I caught them early that morning before I started patrolling. I was just icing them down." These were really just words to fill the air. If a mark on my record was unavoidable I didn't want to prolong the conversation, but I wanted to know why Susan had chosen now to use them.

"Is the schedule acceptable?" I asked to change the subject.

"Should work. You'll be needing to put in some overtime over the weekend with Sportsman's and all."

Allie was going to be disappointed, but there was a six lobster limit. With any luck we could get out early and catch ours, then I could go to work. It was pretty common practice for people to catch their limit, return to shore and place them on ice, and then head out again. That was a line I wasn't going to cross.

"That's fine," I said, hoping that would get me dismissed. He nodded and I left his office. Susan's door was open, and I averted my eyes when I passed. The last thing I wanted to see was the smirk on her face. Remembering the chart in the conference room, I backtracked to my office and opened the door. I waited a few minutes, killing time by checking the tides and weather. It was something Martinez or Susan wouldn't notice, but anyone who lived and fished out here would find it strange. After a few weeks on the water you could read the clouds and currents to determine the weather and the tide charts became like circadian rhythms in your head.

I waited five minutes and left again, leaving the door open behind me in case I needed to make a hasty retreat. After checking the hallway I entered the conference room. The chart was spread on the desk with several Sharpies and papers alongside it. Before I could see what was marked I heard footsteps coming down the hall. There was no time to study the chart, so I reached for my phone, fumbled to open the camera app, and snapped several pictures before turning to leave. I took a quick look down the hall and found it empty. Figuring one of them was in the restroom, I decided to rely on the pictures.

Back at my office, I shut off the light and closed the door. Martinez was still at his desk when I passed, but his back was turned and he was talking on the phone. Susan's office was empty and just as I reached the stairs I heard the restroom door open. I flew down the staircase hoping she hadn't seen me and with a finger over my lips looked over at Mariposa on my way out the door.

I walked quickly to the boat and after checking the water flow against the pilings, saw there was no current so I tossed the lines before climbing aboard. Seconds later, I started the engine and dropped the throttle back into reverse. I couldn't get out of there fast enough, but knew Martinez had a camera pointed at the small marina. Fighting the urge to throttle up, I slipped the lever to the first stop and idled into the channel. I had to be careful now. In the park service boat, I was an example to other boaters—for good and bad. If I ran too fast or cut the corner before a channel marker they would take that as an okay to do it themselves, until it went badly and they grounded—then it was my fault.

As badly as I wanted to see if the pictures revealed anything, I continued to idle to the last marker where I pushed down on the throttle and sped across the flat water toward Adams Key. Usually these rides energized me, but my head was full of "what ifs" and conspiracies and I barely noticed the pristine beauty of the water. I reached the dock twenty minutes later and had to pay my respects to Zero before he would allow me to pass. Finally, I sat at the bar in my kitchen and pulled out my phone. I opened up the pictures and zoomed in on the marks.

They were all along the reef line between Elliot and Sands Key. Whatever those two were hiding was not readily apparent, until I scrolled to the last picture and saw a printed email sitting off to the side.

Chapter 4

Using my fingers, I worked the image of the email into the center of the screen. I didn't recognize the name in the sender field, but I found what I was looking for by studying the email address itself and was surprised to see it was from Florida International University, the site of the bridge collapse. At maximum zoom, the writing became a little fuzzy and I cursed my near forty-year-old eyes as I squinted to read. Justine had been nagging and now with Allie in her corner, I had caved in and bought a pair of drug store readers. They did help, though I kept forgetting where I had left them. I did my best without them and found that part of the page was cut off, but by piecing together what I could see, I discovered it was a request for a memorial for the victims.

My first reaction was that this was a little fast. The accident had only happened yesterday. Then I remembered the equipment already on its way to the site. The faster the debris could be cleaned up, the sooner life would get back to normal for the school. I did a quick Google search for the name on the email, which confirmed that the sender was the president of the university. I had little faith in bureaucrats, but his accomplishments were notable: increasing enrollment and faculty while at the same time improving the graduation rate by double digits. Impressive accomplishments, especially for a state school. He clearly had a plan; unfortunately it appeared to involve Martinez and the park.

I looked back at the chart and the marks along the reef line. Running around four miles off the barrier islands, the reef was actually the northernmost extension of the Florida Keys ecosystem. Famous both for its beauty and danger, the coral heads that reached up to within inches of the surface in some places had been tearing the guts out of unsuspecting ships for centuries. Whether through navigation error or due to the hurricanes that blew through every few decades, captains from the famed Spanish Galleons to pleasure boaters of today had lost their ships and treasures to the reef.

The marks were also in the area I had decided to patrol today. Martinez knew I would be there, although I would be farther offshore than he expected. If the park was involved in providing a memorial of some kind, there was sure to be media coverage; I figured he would be too busy ironing his podium outfit to be analyzing my movements. I didn't think he would take notice. Before leaving my house I got out my paper chart and transferred the marks, then using a ruler transcribed the GPS coordinates from the edge of the page to my notepad. Finally, with a small packed cooler in hand, I headed out the door.

At the bottom of the stairs I paused, looking at

the spinning rods leaning against the house. I left them there, deciding it was too close to the snapper incident to tempt fate—especially since Susan McLeash was involved. Zero must have known that I was heading out and barely lifted his head from his spot on the grass under a shade tree. I nodded to him and hopped down to the deck of the center console.

This time of year it was foolish to head out without first getting a handle on the weather. Out here you didn't need an app or weather station: with an almost uninterrupted three-hundred-sixty-degree view of the horizon, the frequent thunderstorms were easy to identify. You could sit and watch as the anvil-shaped clouds formed. The higher they climbed the more ominous they appeared, and the more dangerous they were.

Like California in the summer, it didn't take a meteorologist to predict the weather. Out west, you had a ninety-five-percent chance of being right if you just called it sunny; here the same odds applied if you predicted a chance of thunderstorms. The challenge was figuring out where they would strike. They were not to be trifled with. Aside from the deadly lightning, the squalls brought blinding rain and winds that quickly kicked up the seas. Today, however, looked fairly benign, with only some small cumulonimbus clouds off in the distance.

Before releasing the lines, I started the engine and entered the lowest number of the marked coordinates into the GPS. I had used the positioning system for years, and longitude and latitude had become second nature. General navigation was easy in the forest, where there were landmarks such as rivers and mountains to mark the direction; here there were the barrier islands, offshore waters, and ever-present skyline of Miami. When all else failed there was the compass mounted on the console right in front of me.

But, in order to find a needle in a haystack you sometimes needed help from the satellites in orbit above us. Looking at the numbers I could extrapolate their position relative to Adams Key and to each other. The first number indicated latitude. With the equator being zero, the higher the number, the farther north the position was. Longitude was expressed by the second number and increased as you moved to the west from its starting point in Greenwich, England.

With the first number entered, I hit the GOTO button. The screen showed a solid line running through Adams and Elliot Keys before heading offshore to the waypoint. But rule number one of navigation was to not rely solely on the GPS. More boaters than I could count had followed the line like it was the gospel and run aground where if they'd used their eyes they would never have gone. I disregarded it for now, released the lines, spun the bow toward Caesar Creek, and headed toward open water.

It was an easy run to the first spot. Though the

GPS could get me within thirty feet, the marks on the chart, especially with the resolution of the picture on my phone, only gave me a general area. Once I arrived I switched the display to the depth finder and started studying the bottom, wondering what I was looking for. The display showed a jagged red line telling me it was live bottom. The coral and sponges below showed as small marks above the bottom and I regretted not taking the fishing gear when I saw the clouds of yellow and green in the water column—those marks were fish. Even if the bottom finder hadn't told me so, I could see from looking over the side by the changes in color that I was over a reef.

The word "memorial" from the email came back to me, and I changed the screen back to the GPS and entered the next coordinates. The wreck Allie, Justine, and I had dove on the other day had occurred naturally, with the ship being taken down by the reef. It still lay where it had been gutted by the coral.

Artificial reefs were placed differently, generally away from established reefs, as their purpose was to create an ecosystem in a new area. Comprised of gutted wrecks and rubble, the man-made reefs had a purpose. Within days they would accumulate a slime coat and in weeks they would become covered with the first layer of growth that eventually would become thick enough for coral and other marine life to grow. Often set into a sandy bottom far from other structures, the reefs attracted resident fish often of the larger variety. It wasn't unusual for some of the resident Goliath grouper and eels to have names. In a year or so, the original structure would be alive. In too many ways, we eradicate vital habitat. This was one safe way to replace some.

The next two areas proved to be more of the same and I was again regretting not bringing fishing gear when I saw a large flock of birds diving on bait right outside of the park's boundary. I only knew it as a line on the chart plotter. Otherwise it was a random division running approximately along the forty-five-foot contour. Several similar lines were displayed farther offshore. The first marked the boundary of the Florida Keys Marine Sanctuary, then the limits of State waters, and finally Federal. Each had their own rules and regulations that confused most boaters, who just ignored them.

The fourth area looked more promising. The park boundary meandered into deeper water here and the depth finder showed sandy bottom running in sixty-five feet—perfect to my eye for an artificial reef. Now that I knew where, the larger question was why was this so top secret. As little as twenty years ago, it had been common practice to dump rubble and call it a reef. The environmentalists had started to regulate, but it was still done. Surely the media would be notified if a memorial ceremony would be held. The only reason I could think of was that this was going to happen quickly and they wanted it in place before the lawsuits and questions started pouring in

I spent the next hour pondering that question while working closer to the shoreline of Elliot Key. After following the mile-long coast I passed Sands Key; finding nothing of note I rounded Boca Chita, the last island in the chain, and turned into the harbor to check my phone. Looking at the boats tied off around the half-filled concrete seawall I pulled up at the end, quickly secured a bow and stern line, and pulled out my phone.

Even on the vibrate mode, it was hard to tell when a call or text was coming in when the boat was running and I saw the screen was full. There was a smiley emoji from Allie. I looked at the time and saw it had been sent during school hours—something I would have to address with her. Having a driver's license hanging over her head made discipline easy. I texted back a quick hello and told her to pay attention, subtly trying to tell her that her dad was no neophyte and I knew when the message had been sent. Another message had come from Martinez. I was surprised that he wanted to know what had brought me offshore, but I ignored that—it would be in my report.

Justine had sent two messages: one when she got back from her paddle and another—I checked the time and saw it was after two—less than a half hour ago. Our communications had been strained since she had been forced to give up the old crime lab where she had tried to stay after the newer lab was completed. Now, surrounded by the day crew until five, she was careful with her personal communication.

The message said to call, which was even more unusual. Hoping everything was okay, I pressed the phone icon and waited for the call to connect. She answered on the second ring.

"Hey," I said. "Everything okay?"

"Hey back. Yeah, it's all good. Just need to get a little perspective from my concrete ninja."

"Happy to help." I wasn't sure what she needed

me for with a high-tech forensics lab at her fingertips.

"They assigned me to the bridge failure and I've got a room full of engineers here. Blood and gore I can handle, but they're talking over my head. I have questions."

I had found a clue from a previous case in the concrete walkway at Boca Chita and given her a brief lesson on spalling at the time. That was a whole lot different from bridge building, but any excuse to see her was a good one and I was done with my patrol. "Sure, if there's dinner involved."

"That would be good."

"You want to pick me up at Dodge?"

"I can be there in thirty minutes. That work?"

My day had taken a turn for the better and I released the lines. I was excited to see Justine, but also curious about the investigation. After passing the last marker, I turned to the north and pressed the throttle down. I had blinders on and almost missed the barge being towed by a tug as I passed under the

Rickenbacker Causeway.

I swerved and turned to avoid the barge, then glanced back and saw the deck was full of debris. My first guess had been correct. The powers-that-be wanted the concrete evidence under the water and out of sight as soon as possible. I thought about following the barge, but I was sure Martinez would see the path of the boat on one of his screens and call me off. I was expecting a call from him, at least wondering why I was taking off early. I rehearsed my excuse again, ready to remind him about the overtime he had asked me to work this weekend. Hopefully he was preoccupied with the memorial. There would likely be national coverage and he would be there front and center when the debris was dumped.

With a nagging feeling that this was moving too fast, I pushed down the throttle and sped toward Dodge Island. Justine was already there and helped me secure the boat.

"They're towing the demolition debris out to

make a reef," I said.

"I heard. They said they have all the samples they need, but this is fast. It's scheduled to be placed with a memorial the day after tomorrow."

I cut the engine, tied off the boat, and hopped up onto the seawall using one of the large tires placed as fenders for the commercial boats that docked here as a foothold. I was anxious now to see what she had found.

Chapter 5

On the way to the crime lab, Justine filled me in on the progress of the investigation. I was surprised that since there was no apparent actual crime the lab would be involved, but there were sure to be lawsuits. Someone had made a deadly and expensive error and the crime lab was well drilled in chain of evidence and conducting impartial investigations. They would probably need outside help, but it made sense that they would be involved.

"You said you had experts in today. What do you need me for?" I asked.

"Did you ever hear an engineer talk about their specialty? It's like they're giving a dissertation to kindergartners. I need some practical knowledge. They can tell me why it failed, but they can't tell me the reason someone would potentially put the project at risk."

"You're assuming this was human error."

"I know the first letters in 'assuming' are a-s-s…"

I let it go, because she was probably right. "The construction industry is a strange beast." It was my turn to give a lecture now. My dad had been a contractor and I had grown up working with him, seeing and hearing a different side of the business. "Construction's a hard deal. It is one of the only businesses where the company has to put a price on something, sign a contract, and produce it before they know what the finished cost is going to be, and won't until after the project is complete."

"What do you mean? Can't you add up the materials and labor?"

"It's not quite that simple," I said, trying not to sound like a know-it-all. "My dad would bid a house from a set of plans then go to the site after being awarded the contract and see that the elevations were wrong and the foundation walls needed to be larger. "

"Can't you get a change order for that?"

"In theory you can, but building a house is often a year-long commitment. Starting a job asking for more money is not going to pay off down the line. If things go badly, you can get the architect involved and they might justify it, but that just starts a slippery slope. It's also not uncommon for the architect to throw the contractor under the bus to cover for their own shortcomings. Once your customers start questioning you, it gets ugly and with the Internet…" I let that thought drift, not wanting to get off course. "Add in unforeseen conditions like rain, snow, heat, and cold, let alone a natural disaster, and you have a Pandora's box. Materials are commodities that go up and down like the stock market, and mistakes are going to be made. A good contractor is more than a builder; the successful ones know how to fix mistakes before they turn into problems."

"Sounds like a hard business."

"It is. Ford knows how much every car is going to cost before they start the production line. The guys building that bridge have no idea until it's complete."

"So, all kinds of stuff can happen between the start and finish of a job."

"Why are they in such a rush to get rid of the debris?" I asked, wanting to end my rant and change the subject.

"I don't know. FIU is on the upswing. I think the fastest way to make this go away is to *make it go away*," Justine said.

I had been so engrossed in the conversation that I hadn't noticed we had reached the lab. She pulled into the partially full parking lot. Checking my watch, I estimated there were about twice as many cars as there usually were at this time of day. "I guess the Ivory Tower is paying overtime for this one."

"Yup," she said, and pulled into a parking space.

"Is it cool for me to come in?" I asked. Without infrastructure of their own, the park service was forced to rely on outside agencies for help. The FDLE was the preferred option, but their closest lab was in Tampa. Most of the time we were forced to use the services of a reluctant Miami-Dade. Justine had helped with several of my earlier cases without kicking it upstairs first, figuring if there was a crime, that was her job, but lately the word had come down that any work for an outside agency needed to be authorized. I had a feeling the policy had come as a direct result of me. This was different, but I had my enemies here and as soon as they saw me coming they would call it in.

"All kinds of people coming and going." Justine seemed to read my mind. "No worries. Just stick with me."

I followed her into the building and waited while she swiped her card in the reader. There were always a few seconds of anxiety before the electronic lock buzzed and we entered through the security door. I looked longingly at the stairs leading down to the old lab and thought of some of the moments we had shared there. Whenever I would come see her I would wait outside the glass window and watch her work to the beat of the music in her headphones. The new lab didn't have a window; the entire wall was solid glass. It wasn't the same, though; the smoked finish revealed little of the interior besides the glow of LED indicator lights from the equipment hitting the shiny stainless steel tables they sat on.

Justine swiped her card again and the thick glass door slid open. The lab was pretty empty. "Where is everyone?"

"Must be a briefing. The project engineers have been here all day."

Justine walked past a row of machines that I had no idea what they were used for. The days of the standard microscope were apparently over. Light shone through the door of what I guessed was a conference room ahead. I followed her to the room and we entered, sliding against the back wall so as not to interrupt the speaker.

Standing at the podium was a woman who could have been Justine's twin if not for her dark hair and complexion. Their bodies both had hard athletic lines and the speaker did little to soften the look, wearing a straight cut business suit that contrasted with the trendy oversized glasses perched on her nose. Behind her a screen showed an image of the rubble after the bridge had failed.

"She's the engineer overseeing the project," Justine whispered.

We stood against the back wall listening. The woman split the screen, one side highlighting sections of the bridge while it was still standing and the other showing close-up pictures after it had failed. She spoke as straight as she looked.

"The tension rods were what failed. It's pretty

clear the contractor didn't follow procedure and tightened them too quickly." She changed slides and put up a graph that was above the pay grade of everyone in the room including me. "Questions?"

It was clear that the assembled group was lost in the engineering. Crime scene techs were trained to find and classify evidence, not analyze failed building components.

"It's always the contractor's fault," I whispered to Justine.

"Well, here's your chance. Prove it's not."

Contractors were far from infallible; in fact they were quite the opposite. This case was probably no different, but it bugged me that the blame was automatically placed there. I could still hear my dad going on about shit rolling downhill, and the incompetence of architects and engineers. But the room was emptying quickly and we soon found ourselves alone with the engineer.

"Did you have a question?" she asked as we

approached.

I stuck out my hand. "Kurt Hunter."

"Roslyn Maya," she said, taking my hand in a hard firm grip. "What can I help you with?"

"Was your company responsible for both the design and testing?" I asked.

"Yes. We've done several of these accelerated bridge construction projects, but mostly in Boston."

Right after the failure, with little real information available, the cable channels had filled their airtime with animated presentations of the ABC techniques. Experts were also brought in to explain the process. I thought I had a handle on the construction process so I focused on the controls.

"Is there testing on the concrete?"

"We have core and slump test samples for every pour, but I can assure you that is not what caused the bridge to fail."

I'd been reading people for years, from the meth heads, illegal dredgers, and poachers out west to the wayward tourists and smugglers here. They all had their own tells and I saw hers right away. Her eyes narrowed, pushing her glasses down her nose when she stared straight at me as if defying me to question her further.

"The samples and results are available at our offices." She pushed her glasses back in place.

"That won't be necessary," Justine answered for me. "As long as you have them. We were just worried that the debris was going to be dumped prematurely."

"It's really quite simple. The contractor went too far, too fast. They would have had to pay liquidated damages if they went past the weekend deadline."

I watched the interaction of the two women. Roslyn's look became even more severe, if that was possible. Justine missed none of this. It was time to get her out of here before the claws came out. "Thank you for your help."

"Any time," she said, with a vague semblance of

a smile. Reaching into her portfolio, she pulled out a business card and handed it to me.

I took the card, pocketed it, and pressed Justine toward the door. "Let's get out of here," I said, wanting to put some distance between the engineer and us. When we reached the hallway she turned to me.

"They're really pushing to place this at the feet of the contractor."

"I get that feeling, too. It's going to take heavy equipment to make her budge. Ditch the evidence and there's not much anyone can say," I said, smelling a cover-up.

"I'd like to look into this accelerated bridge construction thing. See if there were any problems elsewhere."

"FIU had a presentation earlier for the media. It was playing on the closed circuit TV. They're trying to reinforce how safe it is."

"The university and engineers are washing their

hands of any wrongdoing, leaving only the contractor. My dad was right."

"Got your attention now?"

I thought for a minute. "Six people died in the accident, and they're just shuttling blame. This is a murder investigation. If it really was an error then it's manslaughter; if it was intentional it's murder." As I said it I had a moment of lucidity. "And once the crime scene crosses into the park, it's mine."

"See if you can get *that* one past your boss."

"I'll deal with that later. Martinez is just concerned that he gets enough TV time. As long as he's got the spotlight on him, I can wander."

"And how do you intend to do that?"

I didn't have a plan, but now I had an investigation of my own to pursue. Dumping the collapsed bridge in sixty-five feet of water was hiding evidence, and that was a crime being committed in the park.

We both turned toward the glass door leading to

the lobby at the same time. Someone was pounding on the safety glass. It was after hours and the reception desk was empty so I went to the door, thinking it might be a tech that had lost or forgotten their badge. On the other side of the glass stood a man hunched over as if he had the weight of the world on his shoulders. The bags under his eyes told me he hadn't slept in days.

"Can I help you?"

He looked up when he saw me and extended his open palms.

"I got this, special agent," Justine said, and pressed the button on the intercom mounted next to the door. "Who are you?"

"I'm the contractor. Where is that bitch of an engineer?"

Chapter 6

Fighting off the repulsive feeling of his greasy skin, I grabbed the man's arm and led him back out the security door. I wanted him alone.

"Why don't we take a walk," I suggested, continuing to lead him through the small lobby and onto the sidewalk. He started to resist, but I was probably twenty years his junior and easily controlled him. Finally, I had him sitting on the low concrete wall in front of the building. I would have preferred him farther away, but sensed his heart might be as weak as his body.

"Can you keep an eye out for our friend?" I asked Justine.

"Gladly," she said, and turned back toward the entrance.

She went back inside, leaving me alone with the contractor. I waited for a minute while he caught his breath and wasn't surprised when he pulled out a pack of cigarettes and lit one. He inhaled deeply.

"Who the hell are you?"

"Special Agent Kurt Hunter with the National Park Service," I said. My hand was still greasy from grabbing his arm; there was no way I was going to shake his hand.

"Ranger boy, eh." He inhaled again.

I let the comment go. After being here for a year, I was comfortable in my skin. I had been involved in several high-profile cases that were visible enough to get Martinez plenty of podium time and give me a little breathing room as well as the grudging respect of some of Miami-Dade's finest. "Not exactly." I wasn't going to take his sarcasm, nor was I going to justify my position.

"That bitch is trying to frame me," he said, pulling hard on the cigarette and holding the smoke.

Finally he released it and the nicotine seemed to relax him slightly.

Even though Roslyn could walk out the door at any second, I wanted him to talk and stayed silent while he finished the smoke. Finally he ground it out with the heel of his shoe. I studied him while I waited, knowing he would fill the void without me having to ask any questions.

He looked to be in his late sixties, with a blotchy complexion usually caused by drinking, sun, or a combination of both. Dressed in a wrinkled fishing shirt and cargo shorts, he looked like he was ready to step onto a boat or into a golf cart—not a construction site.

"I gotta get to that evidence she's rigging and prove I did everything by the specs."

I had him talking now. "How are you going to prove that? I sat in on her briefing. She's blaming you for accelerating the tensioning of the rods."

"She might be a bitch, but she's smart. Picked

the one thing that can't be proven."

"What are you going to get from the debris? She says there are core samples and tests of the concrete."

"You sound like you know a little about construction."

"My dad was a contractor."

He seemed to look at me in a different light now and relax even more, knowing I was at least part of the same tribe. I knew from growing up around my father and his friends that contractors were different. You had to be part reptile and part lawyer to deal with the customers, subcontractors, and contracts necessary to succeed in a very tough business.

"John Burkett," he said, extending his hand.

I took it reluctantly. "Why don't we take a walk, John?" I asked.

"Rather have a beer," he said.

"We can do that, too. " I got up and looked down at him. He rocked back and forth several times as if building enough momentum to rise. John was not in good shape. "You know a place?"

"Yeah."

"Can I catch a ride with you? I'll get Justine to bring me back."

I didn't think he would mind if she joined us and from the look on his face when I mentioned her name, I was correct. I also wanted her away from Roslyn.

John climbed onto the running board and hauled his heavy frame into the long-bed crew cab pickup. He might not look like a contractor, but his truck did. Complete with chrome running boards, tool boxes, and ladder racks, including the company name and license number on the door, anyone would see him coming a mile away. I climbed into the passenger seat.

John drove conservatively, a habit I suspected he had acquired from experience; being behind the wheel when less than sober. I knew better than to make assumptions, but if it looks like a duck … I had learned it probably is. After about a mile, he turned into a strip center and parked in front of a bar. Before entering I saw a menu posted in a Plexiglas frame to the side. Justine was still on the clock and I realized that I hadn't asked about food earlier and sent her a text so she would know where to find us.

He went for the bar, but thinking about Justine, I steered him to a table. A waitress came over and we ordered beers. I asked for a few menus as well. The half dozen large screen TVs distracted us while we waited for the drinks and just as they were set on the table, Justine walked through the door. She saw us and headed toward the table. John's mood lightened immediately when she sat down. I introduced her and we ordered burgers all around and an iced tea for her. John was already three-quarters through his beer and asked for another.

It was easier to keep him focused with Justine there. Between her looks and his curiosity about her position with the crime lab, John started ignoring me and talking to her. He'd finished the first beer and started into the second when I brought the conversation back to the bridge.

"What do you think you'll learn from the debris?" I asked.

"I don't know, but dumping it before it's even looked at is not going to clear me or my company. The families of two of the people that died have already filed lawsuits. More are sure to follow."

I had learned two things from his last statement and I liked them both. He wanted the truth, and calling the victims "people" showed an empathy that someone deliberately jeopardizing lives by cutting corners would not have. I had to be cautious, though. I'd been fooled by first impressions before, most notably by an FBI agent named Ron Pierce, who'd been running a drug trafficking business on the side. I had liked him initially, too.

"Can't you file an injunction or something?"

"This job has bled me dry. I've been building bridges for years, but mostly for the Department of Transportation. I know the playing field regarding schedules and change orders. But the FIU bridge was overseen by the university, and they fought me tooth and nail for every delay and change, trying to get this done on time and look good for their program."

"Sounds like a conflict of interest," I said, leaving out the fact that a broke contractor was a desperate contractor for further examination.

He tipped his beer mug to me and drained the contents. The waitress arrived with our food and he ordered another. We sat eating while he drank. There was not much more to be said about the bridge until I could do some homework and we let the TVs remove the need for further conversation. After finishing, I picked up the check. Martinez would never reimburse me, but two-thirds of it was for Justine and me.

"I'll see what I can do. You have a number I can

reach you at?" I asked as we were leaving the bar. Instead of handing me a card, he punched my number into his phone and sent me a text that revealed his as the sender. I saved it to my contacts and we said good-bye.

Justine and I stood by her car and watched him leave the parking lot. After three beers and possibly more that I didn't know about, I was worried, but he confirmed my theory and slowly pulled into traffic and drove carefully down the street.

"Well, that was quite the date," Justine said.

"Sorry about that. I wanted to get him at ease with us. I have a feeling there is more to this than a greedy contractor."

"Yeah," Justine said. "But how do we stop them from dumping the evidence?"

"Martinez," I replied. I had been thinking about this and determined there might be some value in his addiction to the podium.

"Really?"

I told her about seeing the chart on the conference room table earlier. "I have to figure out how involved he is besides selecting the site."

"Yeah, good luck with that." She pulled out her phone and Googled the FIU Bridge Memorial. "Says there's already a ceremony planned for the day after tomorrow. You have thirty-six hours to figure it out."

"Thanks for that. I saw the debris being towed out on my way over. Want to take a midnight run and have a look?" I had a feeling she wouldn't be able to resist.

"Deal. Let me go wrap up some things. Should only take an hour."

"Okay if I come back with you?" A few months ago I wouldn't have had to ask. Working the swing shift, Justine had once had total run of the lab after five. But now, between sharing the new lab and the overtime approved by the Ivory Tower we might not be alone.

"The lab is still probably crawling with people.

You'll blend in, especially if that engineer is still there."

"What are you talking about?"

"I saw her looking at you," Justine said.

"Like she wanted to eat me."

"Exactly."

"Maybe we could double date with Roslyn and John." That got a smile from her and I took advantage of the moment and kissed her.

We rode back from the restaurant together. Justine parked. She'd been correct about the amount of people around; there were even a handful of journalists sitting in the waiting area outside the security doors. We fought through the press and I almost had to physically restrain them while she swiped her card. I went back to the lab with her. She had just opened the door to the crime lab when I heard my name called. Turning back, I saw Roslyn standing at the end of the hall.

"Agent Hunter. Got a minute?"

Justine shot bullets at her with her eyes and gave me a weak smile that said to go ahead. She entered the lab and I turned to the engineer. "Sure."

The fake smile was back. "Coffee? There's a lounge here."

I nodded and followed her past the reception area and into a large open space. "Lounge" was a pretty good description for what had been a simple lunchroom in another life. Tired-looking techs and reporters who had made it past the first level of security occupied several of the dozen tables. One wall was filled with state-of-the-art vending machines. We walked up to a futuristic model that made coffee twenty-seven different ways. Roslyn fed a five into the slot and started pushing buttons to customize her blend. When she was finished, I stuck a single in and got six ounces of black coffee. Under normal circumstances my caffeine intake ended early in the morning, but with my planned run out to the bay later, I figured it might not be a bad idea. Roslyn looked like she lived on the stuff.

We sat at one of the vacant tables and I sipped slowly, waiting to see what she wanted. It didn't take long for her to come out with it.

"I saw you talking to John Burkett earlier. Can I ask what your interest in all this is? I wouldn't think a park ranger would have anything to do with a bridge collapse."

In most cases titles were meaningless, but I felt she was being dismissive. "That would be special agent." She was fishing and I fed her the bait. "The bridge is a murder weapon. Six people were killed by someone's negligence—Burkett's, according to you. The evidence is going to be dumped in my jurisdiction. That makes me an interested party."

"Let me tell you about John Burkett."

Chapter 7

Over the next few minutes I got every detail of John Burkett's life except for the answer to the question I really wanted to know: Was he a good contractor? It was alarming how much personal detail Roslyn dragged out and the way she presented it. Her spin was good enough that she could've convinced me that the pope had intentionally killed six people. According to her, Burkett's financial position had caused him to rush the construction, which had resulted in the bridge failure. This was the only fact we could agree on: Burkett had admitted he was having trouble getting change orders approved through the university.

"Was he a good builder?" There's a distinct difference between a builder and a contractor. A builder builds and a contractor contracts. Contractors wear many hats, including builder, but builders are less multi-faceted and have to deal only with the actual construction of the project. A contractor has to deal with workmen's comp, OSHA, contracts, bids, bonds, payroll, subcontractors, and a variety of other tasks.

"He knows his stuff or we wouldn't have used him, but a contractor's only as good as his last job," Roslyn said.

I knew that to be true as well. A multitude of circumstances can change a contractor's performance: drinking, drugs, losing key employees, legal issues, and, often, domestic problems. Contractors are licensed by the individual states, and each state's process creates an individual set of circumstances with the potential for failure. In California, for example, contractors' licenses are fairly easy to obtain, and many carpenters that would likely never reach a position higher than foreman are licensed. This has its own set of pitfalls: bad accounting and financial planning being the most serious. In Florida, the more stringent licensing laws create larger construction companies where the principal, or qualifier, as they are legally known, often never sees a job site.

I already had a sense of how Burkett ran his business, but I still wanted to know if he could build. The answer I got from Roslyn was in the affirmative, making her other statements, clearly throwing him under the bus, seem illogical. His money problems could well have been caused by bad financial planning or bidding, even though in his own view, Burkett thought the university had screwed him out of money on change orders.

That wouldn't affect a good builder in the way he performed his job, though. My dad often said that he would break even or lose money on one in five jobs. There were many reasons for this—usually the customer—but that didn't allow him to cut corners. Whether he made money or not, to him reputation was everything; and Burkett seemed to care about his.

The way we had seated ourselves allowed me a view of the entrance and hallway. Fortunately I was able to see Justine coming toward us before Roslyn did. By the way she was carrying her backpack over her shoulder, I figured she was done working and had come looking for me. I got up as if I had just remembered something important, said a quick good-bye, and walked down the hall where I grabbed Justine's arm and steered her toward the exit. Just as we pushed through the doors, I glanced back and saw Roslyn following.

"What are you doing?" Justine asked, wiggling from my grasp.

"Keeping you out of trouble." For a second I thought she was going to head back inside.

"Got that about right. That woman bothers me."

"I hear you there. She's as two-faced as Susan McLeash and damned near as scary." After listening to her go on about Burkett, I did not want either one of us to fall into Roslyn's crosshairs. "Ready to head out?"

"Lead on, Kimo sabe. I've had enough for one day. Politics takes all the fun out of this job."

We reached her car, where I risked a quick glance at the entrance. There was no sign of Roslyn and I wasted no time getting out of the parking lot. Miami traffic was a no-win situation. The late hour meant there were fewer cars on the road, but night construction on the Turnpike slowed us. Finally, forty minutes later, we reached headquarters. I parked and waved to the camera mounted under the eaves of the building. For what it was worth, I had figured out most of the locations of Martinez's surveillance cameras, but unless I wanted to take some target practice, the best I could do was to let him know that I knew where they were.

We walked together down to the dock. The boat rocked in its slip and I looked around for the source of the waves. Unlike the Pacific, the Atlantic rarely had a noticeable swell unless there was a big storm spinning out at sea. The long-period, two-foot waves were a reminder that we were about to enter the busiest month of hurricane season.

"Better check the weather when we get to your place," Justine said.

She had noticed the waves, too. I had originally thought that with the wind laid down, taking a look at the barge would be easily accomplished in the dark. The way the waves were pushing the boats around in the protected marina I had second thoughts. "Think we might have better luck if we get up early and have a look?"

"Probably better. We can paddle out if you're up to it."

Justine rarely missed a chance to get on a board. She would use mine, leaving me the kayak, which was probably for the better if the seas continued to roll like they were now. I had started paddleboarding and had bought what she called a starter board: wider and shorter than the toothpick profile of her race board. But even with the forgiving design, I was still getting used to balancing in anything except flat water. "You're on."

"That leaves us tonight without an activity, then," she said with a smile.

I leaned in and kissed her, fully aware that we were within view of the camera mounted on a pole at the dock. Releasing her, I grabbed the two lines tied to the cleats on the seawall and hopped aboard. Justine followed and went to the stern, where she grabbed the lines looped over the pilings while I backed out. A minute later we were heading out of the channel.

Once the boat was up on plane, I tilted the engine up slightly until the rpms rose and the bow cut easily through the swell. With Justine leaning against me, I forgot about the bridge investigation. I put my arm around her and pulled her close. For at least a few minutes the world was at peace.

It lasted more than a few minutes; we woke the next morning without Martinez's help. It didn't matter, though: we were up with the sun and had a quick breakfast before carrying the paddleboard and kayak to the dock. Ray is an early riser, and I heard the screen door to his house open only seconds before Zero honed in on Justine. Our departure was delayed slightly while she paid him the requisite attention. While she petted him, I lowered the board and kayak into the water.

With a line looped through the bow and stern handles of the kayak, I used the cleats as resistance to control the descent of the boat into the water several feet below. It was close to high tide now and the operation was easily accomplished. At low tide the drop was close to five feet, making it much harder. I tied one of the lines off and pulled the other free. Using the same procedure I quickly had the board floating next to it. Justine said good-bye to Zero and with our paddles in hand, we climbed down the ladder to the boats.

The weather forecast had shown a low spinning off the Bahamas. That was the cause of the swell, but as long as the wind remained calm it would be an easy paddle out Caesar Creek and into the Atlantic. If I'd been on my own, I probably would have stayed to the inside of the barrier islands, but that was not Justine's way. Between the advantage of the board and her ability, she was ahead of me by a hundred feet and clearly the leader of our expedition in no time.

We paddled northeast, slowly working to deeper water. I had estimated it would be a six-mile paddle, and every twenty minutes I took out my phone, which was protected by a plastic case, and checked our position on the GPS. The water was crystal clear despite the swell, and we were coasting over the shallow patch reefs watching the coral heads in the clear water below when I heard the Darth Vader ring tone. I didn't have to look, and left it in its pouch. Martinez had found us.

I stopped checking the GPS after a few miles, when the outline of the barge became visible. We also stopped taking breaks as the wind had started to put a ripple on the otherwise smooth waves. An hour and fifteen minutes after starting out, we had reached the barge. I was tired, but Justine assured me the wind and swell would make it an easier trip back.

Now that we had reached the barge, I realized for the first time how massive it was. I'd thought the surface would be low to the water and proportionately it was, but it was still above my head. Justine paddled to the anchor line and clipped her leash to the cable. Without saying anything she hopped off the board and into the water with her paddle in hand. She covered the few feet to the barge easily and swam to the stern, where she climbed a welded ladder. I followed her example, taking both my paddle and phone.

We stood staring at the twisted mass of concrete and steel.

"What now, Kimo sabe?"

"You're the tech guru. What do you think?"

"I think we had a good paddle."

It was intimidating standing on a hunk of metal with tons of debris stacked above my head. With every swell, the hull rose and fell, resulting in an eerie creaking sound as the load shifted. I felt like abandoning ship before something shifted and injured one of us, but I also knew this might be our only chance at examining the debris and I wanted to take advantage of it. With no real idea what I was looking for, I started walking around the barge, taking pictures from different angles. Too late, I realized that Martinez was probably watching them come up on his monitor as they streamed from my phone to the Cloud in real time.

It was too late to stop, but my hunch was confirmed when the phone rang again. There was no point in denying I was here and I answered.

"What the hell, Hunter?"

This was the new *hello*. "Just checking out our new reef." The words were out of my mouth before I realized that I wasn't supposed to know about it. "Just out patrolling and I saw the barge inside the park boundary. Thought I'd check it out," I said, trying to cover my tracks.

"You are not authorized to be on that barge."

Justine came by my side and gave me a questioning look. I mouthed *Martinez*.

But then he seemed to relent. "As long as you're out there why don't you check the mooring? I'm a little worried about this low that's forming in the Bahamas.

It sounded like I had dodged a bullet for now, and I disconnected. "Any ideas?"

"You're the concrete ninja." Justine shrugged.

"Yeah, not so much." I was intimidated by the sheer mass of the debris. If we were going to find anything it would take a close examination, but with so much material I wasn't sure where to start.

I decided on top was as good a place as any and started climbing the pile. By the time I reached the summit, my legs were wavering under me. It wasn't fatigue. Standing twenty odd feet above the seas multiplied the effect of each wave and I had to hold on to the debris as the barge moved up and down with each swell.

A larger wave lifted the barge. I lost my balance and dropped to my knees. A piece of exposed steel scraped my knee and I rose to avoid impaling myself on it. On the horizon I saw a boat coming directly toward us. "Justine!" I called.

She climbed to my side and together we stayed low and watched the sportfisher approach. The boat was older, a low-end model for the class of boat, but I knew these cruisers still ran into the mid six-figures. I could make out a single person on the bridge—a man by the look of him—and as the boat approached

I realized it was Burkett.

Chapter 8

The sportfisher came alongside the barge and I watched as Burkett skillfully maneuvered the craft and tied off to two of the oversized cleats protruding from the barge's deck. He climbed over the gunwale, which, already several feet above the water, allowed him easy access to the barge's deck.

He started to prowl through the wreckage, but stopped before he reached our hiding place on the other side of the barge. Grunting as he climbed over the rubble he cursed every thirty seconds or so for the next half hour, then inexplicably gave up his search and returned to his boat. A minute later he was heading back to Miami.

"What do you think he was up to?" Justine asked.

"I don't know, but it's a good thing we brought the board and kayak; otherwise he would have seen us." The five-foot drop to the water from the deck created an angle that, unless you were standing right next to them, hid the boats.

"Didn't seem like he found what he was looking for," Justine said. She rose and started working through the wreckage again.

"He either wanted to find something and couldn't or wanted to make sure no one else would find whatever he was looking for. Fifty-fifty odds."

While Justine climbed through the wreckage I stared at the web of shattered concrete and twisted steel. Whatever Burkett had come looking for could easily have been underneath tons of concrete. We worked our way around to an area where the failed sections of the bridge that were lifted in place lay, and started climbing over it. What had once been a neatly constructed section of the bridge was now rubble.

"Find something?" she asked.

"I should have brought some tools and evidence bags."

Justine reached behind her back and pulled the waist pack she wore that contained a hydration bladder and inflatable PFD around to the front. She separated the velcro seal of a pocket and pulled out a small multi-tool. From the pocket on the other side she removed a Ziploc baggie containing two gel packs. Offering me one, she tore the top from the other and squeezed the contents into her mouth. I followed suit. The carbohydrate-rich mix hit my system in seconds. With the tool in hand, I opened the knife blade and started to scrape chips of concrete from one of the larger pieces.

"That's way too easy," Justine said.

Using the blade of the knife, I dumped several chips into the baggie and moved to one of the exposed sections. It was much harder to chip the finished surface.

"Well?" Justine asked.

Afraid of breaking the knife, I left the exposed area alone and freed several more pieces from the interior section. I would have liked to take a sample of the steel as well, but with only the small tool all I could do was to scrape the rust from the bars.

"Surprised it's not epoxy coated," I told her. The ribbed steel bars known as rebar rusted quickly when exposed to the elements, and the humid South Florida climate was especially destructive to them. Once the steel was encapsulated in plastic, however, it was generally okay; but concrete was porous and if water made its way to the steel the oxidation could expand the bar and break the concrete. Though there was a surprising amount of rust, the barge had only been on the water overnight. I had seen what a night in open water could do to metal and what I was looking at could be a result of the recent exposure to the harsh environment.

"After seeing the inside of this I don't want to

be paddling under any bridges."

"As fast as you are you have nothing to worry about. I'm so slow the bridge could decay and collapse before I passed underneath." I closed the knife, sealed the baggie and handed both to Justine. She put them back in the pockets of her pack. "I don't think there's anything else we can do until the samples can be analyzed."

"I thought your girlfriend, the engineer, said they had tests."

"She did, but I'd prefer my own."

"What are we going to do about the material being dumped tomorrow? It won't be until late tonight that I can get any results, if our equipment can even analyze this stuff."

A larger wave passed underneath the barge and I looked out to the east. "Seems like the seas are building." The sky was still clear and there was no sign of storm clouds. "Maybe that'll help. I've never seen Martinez on a boat—he wobbles on a dock."

"Okay, let's head back," Justine said, and started to climb down. Several other large waves passed under the barge as we descended and I looked back again at the building seas, starting to worry about the six-mile paddle back.

One look at the kayak and barge moving separately convinced me to follow Justine's lead and I dove off the barge with my paddle in hand and stroked hard to the kayak. After squirming aboard, I released the line from the mooring buoy and used the paddle to turn the bow toward land. I struggled and wondered what kind of nightmare I had gotten myself into. Justine was already ahead and I watched as she effortlessly used the swell to her advantage.

I mimicked her movements; she would paddle hard until the momentum of the wave took the board, allowing her a small respite. Though I had nowhere near her experience, I had two blades on my paddle and was able to sit down. She looked back and I could see the smile on her face as another wave lifted the board. After half a dozen hard strokes she had matched its speed and now relaxed, using the energy of the sea to her advantage.

It took me more than a few tries, but I finally got the hang of it. Using my paddle to brace against the waves I started to ride the swells. Soon I found myself in the elusive groove or flow that paddlers and surfers seek, and was shocked when Caesar Creek came up on my right. I followed Justine as she steered her board through the channel. A minute later, I heard Zero greeting us from the dock.

"You did great!" she said.

"That was fun." I reached for the line hanging from the dock and tied off the kayak, then used it to pull myself to the ladder. Once on the dock, I helped Justine. She stepped up the ladder and found herself face to face with Zero when her head reached dock level. With his tongue extended to the max, he stood there pushing forward as far as he dared. I tried to distract him, but he was undeterred, enjoying his moment with Justine.

Finally she pushed up and rose above him. With some attitude, he walked to the grass and collapsed in his shady spot. I guess that was his way of giving us the cold shoulder.

Together we pulled the boats out of the water and carried them to the house. Zero tired of playing hard to get and followed us upstairs.

"You going to try and talk to someone at the university today?" Justine asked.

After showering and making breakfast, we were sitting at the bar that separated the kitchen from the living room. Zero had worked himself between us and lay on the floor, glancing up occasionally for a scrap. I ignored him, but I saw Justine knock a piece of her eggs over the edge. "That's still the plan, but I'm thinking I want someone impartial to have a look at the concrete samples first."

"Probably makes sense. You know anyone?"

"Thought about just finding a random plant and

asking."

"Not very scientific, but those guys work with it everyday. If there's something odd, they'll probably notice. I have to get going. You about ready?"

"Whenever you are." I carried our plates around the counter and into the kitchen, then rinsed them in the sink. Zero came up beside me as I washed them and the pan. I had a dishwasher, but didn't use enough plates to warrant its use. Finally, Zero gave up and went to the bedroom, seeking his last bit of attention from Justine. I finished and went to check my phone before we left. Even on vibrate, it would be pretty much useless while the boat was running.

There were no new notifications and I texted Allie good morning before setting it down. It was a little scary how he seemed to know exactly when to call, but a split second before I set it on the counter it rang.

"You going to work today?" Martinez asked.

"I'm about to head back to headquarters. I think

we should talk if you have a few minutes." It was the last thing I wanted, but I needed to make sure he was on board with me investigating the case. I realized again how well off I'd been out in California with only myself to report to. The special agent in charge there, my boss, had been several hours away. He'd had no choice but to work his own area and pretty much left me alone. Here, I felt stifled by Martinez.

Justine was ready and we headed for the boat. After Zero's longer than necessary good-bye, I idled away from the dock, spun the wheel, and headed toward Bayfront Park. With the wind at our backs it was an easy ride, but it also blew the engine noise back to us, making it hard to talk. I enjoyed our closeness, though I was already preoccupied with how to handle Martinez.

"Can you give me a few minutes?" I asked Justine as we pulled into my slip.

I couldn't help but notice that Susan's boat was here. Apparently it hadn't taken her long to fall back into her old routine—she would likely be sitting behind her desk fine-tuning her latest report. Her boat was tied off, ready for a hurricane, and I realized I had forgotten to check the weather. "Can you see what that low is doing?" I asked Justine while I secured the lines.

She worked her phone, moving through several apps. It was amazing how they disagreed, but I had learned how to compare and take the strong points from each.

"Not really organized and looks like it's moving north."

With the help of our smartphones, everyone in South Florida was a hurricane expert. The forecast was good news and bad. We were not going to get a hurricane, but the show would go on as scheduled. I thought about embellishing the weather angle, but Martinez would see through it. Weather affected his budget; he knew what to look for.

Justine and I parted ways at the top of the

walkway leading to the dock. She went to the right, where her car was parked; I went for the main entrance. Mariposa greeted me with a warm hello.

“How’s the boss?”

“Him and that Susan have been all secretive. You know what’s going on with them?” she asked.

I was surprised that for once I knew more than she did. If anyone wanted to know what was going on here, Mariposa was usually a clearinghouse of schedules, rumors, and gossip. Unlike our boss, she did it the old-fashioned way, by building relationships.

“I’ll fill you in on the way down.” Normally I would delay heading into his lair as long as possible, but this morning it was me who wanted something from him. I climbed the stairs, rehearsing what I planned to say. That all fell apart as soon as I saw Susan sitting in her usual chair by his desk.

“Moorings secure?” he asked, motioning me to the other chair.

I confirmed that they were and slid by Susan. From my customary seat I glanced over at the monitors. Two had feeds from the security cameras—one carried a close-up of the parking lot and I thought he might have something to say about Justine being here. The last screen that I glanced at before he started talking had a satellite view of the storm.

"Big news, Hunter," he said.

I played dumb, but did not fail to notice he was in his podium uniform. "What's that?"

"Biscayne Bay National Park is about to get a new artificial reef."

He seemed awfully pleased with himself. "I kind of figured that out." It was time to burst his bubble. "You realize that leaves us with a murder scene at the park."

"What are you talking about?" Susan asked, turning toward me with a hateful look.

"Whatever caused that bridge to fail, even if it

was accidental, is manslaughter. The bridge didn't just fail on its own—someone caused it."

"The University wants to put this behind them and dedicate the wreckage as a memorial."

"Of course they do," I said, under my breath.

"What does that mean? This is a big deal for the park. Artificial reefs are known fish attractors and placing it in sixty feet of water with mooring balls surrounding it will allow divers access."

I figured it would be a boon for his budget as well, but not much else. I was all for artificial reefs. We had destroyed enough natural habitat. I knew that as long as the debris was clean, it would quickly become a sanctuary. "We can't just let them dump it without an investigation," I argued.

"Be that as it may. The engineer is saying it's the contractor's fault and we're dumping the debris tomorrow morning." He opened a file and handed me a piece of paper. "This is your assignment."

Chapter 9

Sitting in Martinez's office with him and Susan staring at me I had no choice but to look at the paper he had just handed me. It was a schedule of events. Text marked with yellow highlighter indicated my responsibilities. I scanned the other items and saw he and Susan were handling the ceremony. If they were the chef and maitre d' in this restaurant, I was in charge of valet parking.

With the media already alerted, there was no delaying the inevitable in his mind. Unless I could find someone higher up the food chain, the evidence would be sitting in a pile on the seafloor by tomorrow morning. I suspected Burkett had a plan to sabotage the ceremony, but I was not ready to team up with him. Burkett had no power and Roslyn would have dumped the evidence already if it had been up to her. The university was the next and possibly the last rung on the ladder.

With nothing else to be gained by staying, I took the paper, nodded to Martinez, and left the office. After a quick stop to confirm our next dinner with Mariposa, her husband, and his Appleton 21, I asked her to keep me posted on the plans for the ceremony and headed to the truck.

Justine sat in her car with the door opened. I hadn't expected her to still be here. She was deep into her phone.

"From the look on your face, I'm not going to ask you how it went."

"Yeah. They don't care about anything except the media coverage."

"Have you talked to Allie since the other night?"

"Just a quick hello. What's up?"

"I think she's having some trouble processing all this."

"You talking to her now?"

"Yup."

"What about school?" I asked. Her look reminded me it was summer break. I remembered my text conversation yesterday where I had accused her of texting from school. It was hard to stay in tune as a weekend parent, but I knew I should do better. "What can I do?"

Another patented look. "Maybe talk to her?"

I promised to, but I wanted to get out of here first. "You need to get to work?" I asked, trying to change the subject.

"Right. What's your plan?"

"Concrete plant and then the University. I've got to try and convince someone to not dump that debris."

"What about Burkett?"

"I guess it's time to bring Miami-Dade in."

"Sounds good. How about if we split the concrete sample and I'll see what I can come up with on my end?" She reached into her backpack and took out a pair of gloves, then sorted the concrete chips between two evidence bags.

"You going to have any trouble with your bosses if you're doing this?" The word had come down from the Ivory Tower that working for me was off-limits unless it had a Miami-Dade case number attached to it. There were, of course, ways around it, but most involved Martinez.

"Not this time. We were brought in as consultants. It's already on the board and they're billing hours. Anything they can do to accrue charges and cover their butts they will."

"I thought the National Transportation Safety Board had authority in these kinds of cases." Come to think of it, I had wondered about why I hadn't seen any of their iconic windbreakers around.

"The University is to Dade County like Vatican City is to Rome. Even though the church is in Rome, the locals have no jurisdiction. Same thing here. The University is state property, but inside the county, and with the Accelerated Bridge Construction program based there, they plan to do their own investigation." She sounded as if she was reciting the contents of a memo from above.

"That's a conflict of interest. They'll be sued," I said.

"I heard papers had already been filed."

It was a sad statement about society that we both *assumed* there would be lawsuits, and the major thrust of some of the agencies that had the resources to solve the case, mainly the University and Miami-Dade, were more worried about liability than the truth.

I wanted to change the subject from work. "Mariposa is after us for another dinner. You up for that?"

"Yeah, I like them," she said.

There was something in the way she spoke that sent alarm bells ringing in my head and made me start to think. We had spent almost the entire last day together and talked about little besides business. "Maybe we can plan a weekend somewhere?" I asked.

"Now that would be good." She slid her hand out the door and we locked fingers.

That should have made me feel better, but it had the opposite effect. I knew better than to mix business and pleasure and had sworn to myself that I wouldn't let work get in the way of our relationship, yet I kept letting it happen. I also knew that once I had a case, I couldn't focus on anything else. Justine was like that in her own way as well. Her paddle time was sacred, and when she was onto something at work it was similar to watching a dog with a bone. I knew that didn't justify my actions, though, and swore once again to be better and try harder. But I had said it so many times now it felt hollow, and my mood darkened.

She must have sensed it. "Can I take you to dinner later?" I asked. If I was going to change I figured I had better start now.

"Yeah, that'd be good if you have time."

"I'll make time," I said, leaning into the car and kissing her hard. It was a long kiss, the kind that usually led to other things, but that would have to wait until later. Justine closed the door and gave me a smile that told me I was on the right track. I watched as she pulled out of the parking lot, until the car disappeared onto the mangrove-lined road. I went to my truck and moved under a shade tree, pulled out my phone and started to search the local concrete plants. There were several nearby; one in particular was close to FIU. After entering the address in the maps app, I followed the directions to the plant.

Located west of the Turnpike, the plant looked more like a mining operation than I'd expected. Dredges were working a large lake that had an unnatural tinge to it. If the color of the water could have been named like a paint color, it would have been nuclear green. The plant office was in a low concrete-block building near the front. After seeing the color of that water, I had mixed feelings about the flagpole proudly flying the American flag in a poorly landscaped island in front of the entrance. I found a lone shade tree by the side of the lot and parked.

A banner attached to the wall underneath the weather-worn *Brockmore Concrete* sign said they worked weekends and I wondered, after seeing the state of the property and as I entered the fifties-style lobby, if they were hurting for money. The interior of the building was as austere as the exterior and a receptionist that might have been there since it was first constructed greeted me. I showed her my credentials and asked to see the plant manager.

I wasn't sure what I'd expected a concrete man to look like, but the man that came through the door behind the reception counter was not it. Dark-skinned and trim, there was something about his look and the way he held himself that said cocky, if not arrogant. I tried not to judge as he walked toward me with his hand extended.

"Albert Brockmore. I'm the owner." His handshake was firm.

"Kurt Hunter, Special Agent with the National Parks Service."

"Didn't know they had special agents in charge of procurement now. You from the Everglades or Biscayne?"

"Biscayne."

"Used to deal with this guy named Martinez over there. Park service sure likes their concrete. You guys paid for my boat." He laughed. "Stopped bidding the work, though."

We at least agreed that the park service liked concrete and I couldn't leave the Martinez comment sitting there. "What happened?"

"Too hard to get paid. That guy had excuses for everything. Learned a long time ago in this business that when someone's favorite word is 'budget', you'd better watch your receivables."

"Somewhere we can talk? I have something I'd like to get your opinion on." He looked skeptical, but led me back to his office. From the pictures on the wall—exotic vacations, boats, fish, women, and a few older shots of what looked like a military unit—I guessed the concrete business had been good to Brockmore. I scanned the photos on the wall, seeing Albert and a man that looked like he might be his father standing on the transom of a boat holding several large fish.

"Nice fish. That the boat you were talking about?" The name on the transom was *Mud Man.*

"I was only kidding, but yes. What can I help you with?" he asked.

I got the feeling he was soured on the park service and sat down. I pulled the evidence bag from my pocket and handed it to him. "Anything you can tell me from looking at that?"

"You'll have to tell me where that's from and

what you're after first. I wouldn't put it past Martinez to send you out here with a sample from the park and have me incriminate myself."

This was going to be too easy. "I wouldn't put it past him, either. This is from the FIU bridge that collapsed." I seemed to have his attention now and he reached for the bag.

"I can tell you what's wrong with that mix without even looking at it." He motioned me to sit. "See how that crumbles?" He worked the bag with his fingers.

"Does that mean the concrete's defective?"

"'Defective' means there is something wrong with it. I believe that was batched to the specs. That bridge-building program at the school called them out. You know anything about concrete?"

"A little, but I'm good if you start from the beginning." I took out a notepad.

"Batching concrete is all about your recipes. Different applications have different ratios of materials. You generally have the same ingredients, but the proportions change."

He continued on with a list of aggregates and what factors changed their quantities in the mix. I wrote down the key stuff, but knew most of the information was available on the Internet.

"Now, that job called for a whole lot of fly ash in place of cement. Those greenies over at FIU spec'd the stuff. It was enough that I refused to bid the project."

"What's the fly ash do?"

"It's a byproduct of burning coal. The good stuff comes from power plants, of which we have a ready supply from Turkey Point. But you have to be careful where you use it."

I already knew a bit about the nuclear plant located on the shores of the park. A body had turned up among the miles of cooling channels there, on my watch. They also had a conventional coal-burning plant there. I nodded for him to continue.

"In many cases it can work as a green solution. It's a substitute for Portland cement, which is not exactly environmentally friendly."

I looked out the window at the bright green lake and I couldn't help but wonder what "environmentally friendly" meant to him.

He continued. "Portland's still the best stuff, though. Fly ash can be substituted if you're careful; maybe for a slab or sidewalks. If it's done right for structural stuff it can work, but there are a lot of variables."

"Like what?"

"Water is the big one. Also some of the additives can change things. In this case it was the schedule. If you want the necessary strength with the mix they specified, it takes a lot longer than the standard twenty-eight days for it to cure to strength."

I wrote down "twenty-eight" and underlined it. "Kind of goes against the premise of an accelerated bridge schedule."

"Like I said, those pinheads at the university wanted it both ways: green and fast."

I remembered my dad talking about a triangle he used to use to explain the construction process to potential clients. The three points were cost, time, and quality. His point was that you could have two, but not all three. Achieving fast, good, and cheap at the same time sounded about the same as accelerated and green.

I thanked Albert and headed out the door. I had the distinct feeling as I walked to my car that he was relieved to see me go.

Before leaving for my next stop, I checked my messages and saw one from Justine: *Call your daughter.*

Chapter 10

I called Allie on my way to FIU. For the first time since we had re-established our relationship I was glad when it went to voicemail. I left a message and sent a text as well to ease my guilt, but still felt like I was letting her down. In order to process the disasters in our lives we need answers. I felt I was getting closer to the truth; maybe that would help us both.

It might have been the doldrums of July, but the campus was still busy. Remembering the enrollment numbers from the school's website, I guessed the summer sessions were just as busy as those of the fall and spring. I turned into the campus and followed the signs to the engineering school. There were several open parking spaces in the adjacent lot and I wondered if my park service truck would allow me to park without a visitor's pass. That decision was a no-win for me, and I walked over to the kiosk and bought a daily parking pass. Pocketing the receipt I went back to the truck and placed the ticket on the dashboard. Martinez was going to get this one, and he would probably tell me I could have parked for free, but it wasn't worth incurring his wrath if instead he had to add a parking ticket to his budget.

I had another choice to make: go to the administration offices and ask for a sit-down with the dean, or wander around and see if I could get a feel for the place on my own. I chose the latter.

Allie made my cover easier when she called back. I sat down on a bench near the entrance where several other people were talking or texting, and answered. I tried to read her from the tone of the conversation and knew immediately she was upset by the breakneck speed she was using to relay her last few days' activities. It was Allie's thing to talk faster when she was nervous and I let her go until she ran out of steam.

"How are you feeling about the bridge collapse?"

"I keep thinking about it. I know we weren't even close enough to see it, but another minute and we would have been underneath it."

There was an easy answer, which I avoided. I didn't want to preach—her mother did enough of that. Not being particularly religious, I wasn't going to tell her it was God's wish. That might seem an easy way out, until you had to explain the converse and find a reason why others had been killed instead.

"We were just lucky, I guess." It was a non-answer, but all I had. Epictetus, one of the stoics, believed that you should imagine your death every day. One of their tenets was that death is inevitable; it's just the details that we don't know. But try explaining that to a fifteen-year-old.

"Are you worried about something like that when you start driving?"

"What if that happens?" she asked.

I thought that I had found the problem. "You know there's stuff you can control and other stuff you can't."

"Sure, but stuff seems to happen around you." She paused. "Sorry, I didn't mean it that way."

My heart sank at being called a shit magnet by my kid. It had to be Jane talking. "No worries." I could confirm that tendency, and tried to justify it with a Hunter S. Thompson quote that if it made your blood boil it was probably worth doing.

"I get that, but please be careful," Allie said.

"You know it." We talked for a few more minutes about our next visit. I hoped the conversation had helped and disconnected. Jane had been generally cooperative in our new joint-custody relationship, but apparently she was still grinding her axe. I would have to think of a way to tell her the blade was sharp enough that when she used it, it cut deeper than she intended.

I sat for a few more minutes watching the students and faculty pass by. It was hard to believe that Allie would be at school in just a few years. We had even started to talk about a road trip to Gainesville. The students looked so much older and I guessed there were going to be a lot more conversations like the one we'd just had before she graduated.

People-watching was interesting, but not helping my case any. I needed to find someone to talk to and so I entered the building behind a group of nerdy-looking coeds. "You guys know where the Accelerated Bridge Construction program is?"

They stopped and looked at my uniform. "The artificial reef is being handled by the marine biology department."

"I was interested in talking to someone about the program in general. You know, maybe get some background on how this all works so I can fill in the tour groups." It was a small lie.

"Sure, man. Follow us. We're headed there now. You ought to check out the Wall of Wind, too."

I had heard about the hurricane simulator. "Maybe next time," I said, following them through a pair of large double doors. I barely made it through the door when a security guard stepped in my path.

"Something I can help you with?" he asked, revealing a gold tooth as he smiled.

I don't often feel small at six feet, but he stood a good half-foot above me and was so wide that I could no longer see the group I had come in with. The bleach-tipped dreadlocks and the stubble on his face, in what looked like an attempt to grow a beard, pegged him as a football player. Before I could answer, a smaller man scurried toward us. He was the opposite body size and type, and from my experience probably considerably more dangerous.

I couldn't help but notice the smaller man's belt. Besides his sidearm, where his hand fell, he had a taser, a mag light, and a radio. There was no badge per se, but there was an embroidered shield on his uniform shirt and he wore a name tag. I'd seen his type before, and knew the weight of all the stuff he carried on his belt still weighed less than the chip on his shoulder.

I pulled out my credentials and handed them to him, knowing he wouldn't just accept a quick glance. He studied them for a minute and turned away. I heard my name mentioned as he spoke into the microphone clipped on his lapel. I looked over at the football player, who appeared bored and ready for a snack.

"Agent Hunter, do you have an appointment?" He handed the wallet back to me.

"No, just looking for some information on the specifications for the concrete used in the bridge." There was no reason to call out which bridge. The beefed-up security was enough to tell me they were on high alert. I had hoped by being specific I might be able to talk to someone.

"Sorry, can't help you without clearance. I hope you can appreciate the sensitivity of this matter."

I couldn't, but he was not the one to voice my opinion to. "If you have a library, maybe I could do a little research without bothering anyone." He seemed to think for a minute and asked the other guard to escort me to room 112. Without another word, he turned away and walked down a hall and around a corner.

"Come on. I'll take you over there."

It was awkward following the larger man. The corridor was too narrow to walk side by side and with him in front I couldn't see where I was going. After making several turns he opened the door to a room. It was larger than I'd expected, with bookcases lining the walls and long tables in the center like an old-fashioned library. Assuming I had been given the run of the place, I went to the far wall, where there were racks holding blueprints.

Each set of plans was held by a metal bar with

the project name on it, making it easy to scan through them. Organized by date from left to right, they started in the early 2000s with several projects and increased through the years. I walked to the last rack on the right to find the most current plans. An empty spot in the rack showed me where I guessed the FIU bridge plans had been stored.

I grabbed the set next to the open spot, a plan for a bridge in Boston, and took it to one of the long tables. Laying the set out flat, I started leafing through the pages. The first dozen sheets were the civil engineering and site plans. Toward the middle of the set were the foundation and structural plans. I stared at the pages, full of small type and drawings, feeling as if I was looking at a foreign language. House plans were the extent of my blueprint reading experience; I would need help to find the concrete specs I was looking for.

"You look confused," the guard said.

"A little over my pay grade." I was about to

close the plan when he stepped next to me.

"Something specific you're looking for?"

"Concrete specs, I think."

He motioned to the plans and I slid over to make room. The two-by-three-foot pages looked like a paperback in his hands as he thumbed through them.

"Here's the mix, curing times, and testing requirements." He pointed one large finger toward some small text.

I leaned closer, but my almost-forty eyes were no match for the fine print. "Does anyone actually read these?" I was familiar with boilerplate specifications from house plans. They were typically the same for every set an architect produced, or at least similar enough to get you in trouble for not reading them.

"You know us engineers. Life is in the details. Now, you came all the way out here to find something; maybe I can help."

I had nothing to lose. "I did a visual inspection of the debris they are planning on dumping tomorrow and found it was kind of brittle. One of the concrete plants confirmed that it was due to the specifications calling for a large amount of fly ash to be substituted for Portland cement."

He looked around the empty room. "Environmental Studies people have been after us to make all things greener."

"From my experience there are a lot of unintended consequences from doing that."

"Designing with new materials scares the crap out of me." He looked at the door.

I saw someone in the hallway start to pass by the door, then linger for several seconds. It was the other guard. "You want to get a bite to eat?" I asked, thinking that was an offer that wasn't going to get turned down. Between food and privacy I thought I might be able to get some good information.

He nodded and grabbed the radio clipped to his

belt. I noticed he had none of the other stuff that the other guard had, making me think this was a temporary assignment for him. After being granted a lunch break, he confirmed that he was escorting me out of the building and showed his gold tooth when he smiled and led me to the door. In one move, he had gotten his boss off his back by getting me off the premises and a free lunch.

We left the building and I started to the truck.

"We can walk. Burger place just around the block."

"That'll work. What's your name?"

"Willis and yes, I play offensive tackle for the football team. Also, Deans List for engineering."

I had my man.

Chapter 11

My one thought as I watched Willis eat was that Martinez was going to cover this bill. With the receipt firmly ensconced in my wallet, I took one bite to his three. This was in proportion with our order: one burger for me and three for him, plus fries of course. I had started to ask questions as we ate, but he didn't seem to want to be bothered by conversation. I let him go, hoping the wait would be worth it. It wasn't that long before he pushed aside the tray, which by then contained nothing but a few grains of salt and paper wrappers. I took my last bite and organized my thoughts. I suspected I had an ally, especially after feeding him, but I also knew he was still a student and employee of the school and had to respect that. I took out my pad and pen, then glanced over at him to make sure it was okay. He nodded and took a long pull on his soda.

"How's the football team looking?" I asked, not really caring for their status, but more to find out if he was on scholarship. I had seen the seedier side of college football on another case involving recruits and boosters. Willis didn't seem like the kids involved in that case, though. They'd clearly not been engineering students, only looking to go to college to party and as a stepping-stone to the NFL. Players who actually took the school part of college football seriously had my deepest respect. It was a grueling workload of practices, travel, games, and class. I was not going to endanger Willis's scholarship by coercing him into talking—unless of course, he wanted to.

"Fair to good, I'd say. We've got a lot better over the last few seasons. Coach Davis got us to a bowl this year."

He sounded proud. "That the same Butch Davis

who coached Miami?" I had heard the high-profile coach had returned to South Florida after several mediocre seasons at other schools.

"Yeah, we had a winning record last year. Hoping to get off to a good start again."

"You a senior then?"

"Graduate student. This is technically my fifth year. When I started as a freshman here, they didn't redshirt anyone. Then I blew my knee out sophomore year. The NCAA gave me another year of eligibility."

I was glad the rules had worked for someone. "You on scholarship?"

"FIU's been good to me. They could have put me out after my knee and all, but they let me stay on."

"Any shot at the pros?"

"Nah. Believe it or not, they say I'm undersized. A little too slow, too. I'm good with it. I got the education that I came here for."

It made me feel good that some colleges cared about their student athletes and that the system had worked for someone. "Engineering your major?"

"Mechanical is my specialty."

I was kind of glad he wasn't in the Accelerated Bridge program. "I don't want you to get in trouble here, but do you have any thoughts on the bridge failure?"

"My minor is in environmental studies, so I kind of have a unique perspective on things."

"The added fly ash in the concrete; I heard that came from the environmental people."

"Here's the thing. The environmental studies people come in two varieties. Most are the Save-the-Earth crowd and will probably end up working for the government in the hope of shutting down the second group, who will work for the companies trying to develop sensitive projects. This 'fly ash thing' was hotly debated." He raised both hands palms up, like he didn't understand.

"And as an engineer you have a problem with this."

"You got that right. It's all good trying new techniques and new materials, but mixing them together is foolish."

"How so?"

"You don't know what really failed, like with this bridge. They've been using the technique for a while, but it's still not perfect. By introducing the fly ash into the mix it's impossible to tell if it was the technique that failed or the material."

I could tell from the way he talked that he would be a good engineer. He had a rare perspective, especially for someone so young. "It sounds like you have some field experience."

"I worked for a testing company the last two summers. They're boosters, so they let me work around my practice schedule."

"You ever test concrete?"

"Mostly did geotechnical tests like compaction

and that sort of thing. You don't need as much experience to run the thumpers and those suckers are heavy. Kind of in my wheelhouse."

"Don't you need to be a certified engineer to do the testing?"

"The licensed guys are supposed to oversee and have to approve the findings, but they seldom come out for the actual tests unless it's an observation."

That sounded like it could be sketchy having student employees doing the testing. "Anyone ever make mistakes?"

"Kind of why I'm specializing in mechanical. Earthwork and concrete are fuzzy math. Too many variables."

He was the second person today to say almost the same thing. "What kind of variables?"

"I'm assuming you're asking about concrete specifically?"

I nodded and opened my pad. Before he could answer, a blast of hot humid air blew in from the door. Willis was facing the entrance and I could see from his face that he was in trouble. I turned to look and saw the security guard leading Roslyn into the restaurant. From the look on their faces they weren't here on a date.

"Even though we lost, getting to a bowl game was the highlight of my career. " Willis said loud enough that they could overhear.

I quickly put my pen and pad away and tried to relax.

"Thought you were going to lunch." The security guard stood with his hands on his hips by the table.

Willis spread his hands out over the empty tray.

"If you told him anything…" Roslyn started.

"We were just talking football. I like to support real student athletes," I said.

"Big FIU fan, are you?" the security guard asked.

He wasn't expecting an answer and I wasn't giving one. "You want some dessert or anything?" I asked Willis.

"Willis is done giving interviews," the guard said bitterly.

I was done as well and stood. Willis took my lead and moved away as if blocking for me. His bulk moved the pair away from the table.

"Can we have a word?" Roslyn asked, fighting past him like a linebacker.

I figured she had forgotten my name and I wasn't going to make it easier for her. "Say hey to Coach Davis." I said it like we were long lost buddies.

"Will do. Thanks for the lunch. Let me know what game you can make and I'll have some tickets at will call for you."

I was glad we had talked a little about the team before getting into the engineering. We almost sounded sincere. I pulled a card out, wrote my cell number on the back, and handed it to him. My reflexes kicked in and before I thought about it, I almost blurted out to call me if he had any more information, but held my tongue. "If you need anything give me a shout."

He walked out of the restaurant leaving a void as large as his body. Roslyn took his chair and pulled it close to the table. I sat back down. The security guard, not sure what to do, looked outside. Once Willis was far enough away that he wouldn't have to interact with him he said good-bye to Roslyn, gave me a nasty look, and took off. Sitting across from the engineer I wondered what she wanted.

"Those students don't always understand all the parameters of a project."

I guessed she hadn't bought my ruse that we were having a football lunch. There was no need for a response; I felt the rant coming.

"So, can you tell me why the National Park Service is so interested in this tragedy?"

There are some times when you are best served by telling the unvarnished truth. Martinez had been so busy preparing his speech and preening for the ceremony that he had failed to either call me off the case or authorize me to work it. I had nothing to lose and if I was going to get any answers, I needed her to show me a little respect at the minimum and a dose of fear wouldn't hurt either.

"The University has decided to ditch the evidence from a murder under sixty feet of water."

"That's a stretch," she said.

"Hardly. Dumping the evidence in the Atlantic tomorrow is a rush job in any book. If the NTSB had any authority over this tragedy they would never allow it."

"Plodding bunch of fools. We know what caused the failure. It's clear the contractor used too much force too quickly on the tension rods."

"Wouldn't that be relative to the strength of the concrete at the time he did it? Post twenty-eight days, that concrete should have cured out to about ninety-eight percent of its compressive strength. Maybe the amount of fly ash introduced to the mix had something to do with it." I watched her face and saw the slightest trace of a smile around her eyes.

"You are an interesting one for a park ranger."

"Special Agent." I don't often correct people, but I needed every ounce of authority I could cling to.

"Why don't you be the good guy here and delay the ceremony? Take some time and find out what the real cause of the failure was."

"Overtightened tension rods."

"And not even the possibility of any other mitigating circumstances?"

"Special Agent. I have been an engineer for twenty years. I am not a graduate student on a football scholarship."

We appeared to be at a standoff and there was nothing more to be gained by this discussion. "I have no doubt about your qualifications as an engineer, but what happens to Burkett? He's going to get strung up for this."

"If that's what he deserves." She got up and left.

I sat there for a minute breathing deeply, hoping that it would bring my blood pressure down. Roslyn also had twenty years' experience in pushing people around and she was good at it. I had stood my ground, but it had been like taking several body blows in a boxing match. I walked to the counter, refilled my water cup, and sat back down with my phone. It was getting to be mid-afternoon and I felt like I was spinning my wheels.

I often use a virtual jigsaw puzzle to figure out crimes. You had to find the four corners: motive, means, opportunity; and the trigger incident that pushed the perpetrator to commit the crime needed to be identified and put in place before you could start working on the border and interior. As the puzzle became filled in the possibilities decreased. But I was frustrated, still struggling with the corners.

Glancing down at my watch, I saw it was after

two. Justine would be at work. If there was anyone that could make lemonade out of lemons it was Justine. I just needed an excuse to get into the lab. I reached for the phone, thinking of a pretext, and jumped when it vibrated. A glance at the screen showed that I had not fallen off Martinez's radar; I appeared to be in the bullseye. Knowing I would only be digging a deeper hole for myself if l didn't answer, I rose and left the restaurant before answering.

"What the hell, Hunter?"

It was his standard greeting these days. "Just running down some leads."

"I got a call from the engineer that you're trying to get the ceremony pushed back. Let me tell you loud and clear—that is not going to happen."

If that was all he was concerned with I would take it as a win. They might dump the evidence, but I still had a case.

"And Hunter. You've just spent your day off up there. Go see your girlfriend and get back to work."

Chapter 12

Even though I knew he meant it differently, Martinez had instructed me to see my girlfriend, so I intended to take him up on it. I loosely interpreted his suggestion to mean I had reason to visit the crime lab.

I pulled out my phone and sent a quick text to Justine that I had some questions and that Martinez had authorized me to come by.

I headed over to the lab and parked in the crowded lot. From the line of news vans parked along the driveway I guessed nothing else had come up in the news to supplant the bridge collapse. Martinez would be happy if the trend continued overnight, with the media giving the ceremony its full attention. But that also made my goal of getting the ceremony delayed that much harder. Reporters were milling around the front of the building, clogging the small entrance. I wasn't sure what the attraction was, unless Roslyn was giving another *reveal nothing* press conference. Forensics work, despite recent glamorous portrayals in the *CSI Wherever* shows, was detailed work; paint drying was often more exciting.

One of the reporters must have noticed my uniform. After calling his camera man away from chatting up a colleague, he approached me.

"How does the National Park Service feel about the new artificial reef?"

I dodged the camera and made it to the door, where I entered the visitor's code that Justine had given me. After a long pause, the electronic lock released with a buzz and I pushed the door open before the reporter, and more importantly the camera man, could reach me. If I wanted things to go badly for me, showing up representing the park service on TV was a surefire way to incur Martinez's ire.

I took several wary looks behind me to see if I

was being followed as I walked down the hall to the crime lab. The corridor was clear. My imagination was working overtime. After several deep breaths I called Justine, who came to the smoked glass doors and let me in.

"Hey," she said, turning and leading me back to her workstation.

I missed the days when I could watch her jamming to the too-loud music in her headphones from behind the glass partition in the old lab. I'd often watched her body swaying under the loose-fitting lab coat for minutes before entering. Now, the headphones were gone and so was the intimacy we'd shared.

"What'cha got?" she asked.

"Martinez told me to see my girlfriend, so I am taking him literally and here I am." She looked around. I wasn't here to get her in trouble, but I had no real agenda. "Maybe, if you don't mind, we could examine the samples we took from the barge. I've gotten several lessons in concrete mixes and engineering today."

"Oh, do tell." She moved to a table where the concrete chips lay.

"Did you have a chance to look at them?"

"Believe it or not, we had a few crime scenes to process today."

"I didn't mean it like that. I'm probably the only one that cares about Burkett being railroaded."

"Truth, justice, and the American way. Pretty cool I have my own Clark Kent." She looked around the room like she had a secret. "And his super powers." She reached over and smacked my arm. "You still think Burkett is innocent after his visit to the barge? He's certainly acting like he has something to hide."

"I have to agree with you there, but they all do. FIU has a bunch of rent-a-cops running around the engineering department and Roslyn seems to know where I am every minute of the day." I gave her a quick rundown of meeting Willis and my conversation with Roslyn in the restaurant.

"One of my professors told us that science is as much an art as a problem you can work out on a slide rule. I guess engineering is the same."

"And the pursuit of the truth gets put on the back burner as they all try and cover their butts." The bridge failure was turning into as much a study on the shortcomings of the human race as the failure of a concrete mix. "Can we have a look at the material?"

"Sure." She handed me a pair of gloves and put on her own. "What are you looking for?"

"I guess it's one of those things that I won't know until I see it." I started moving around the pieces of concrete, rubbing a few between my fingers. Some crumbled to my touch; others resisted and held firm. As I moved the pieces around I thought back to the irrigation pipe I had found in the stream out west, the one that had changed my life. It had defied nature; its small current had taken my fly in the wrong direction through an eddy that alerted me that something was wrong. Straight lines, even well-camouflaged ones, were not found in nature, and the pipe caught my eye and led me to work my way uphill to the pot grow.

The concrete I held was manmade, but still a mix of natural materials. The loose mix would conform to the surfaces that contained it until it cured, and the only smooth and perfect features of it would be left from the forms. As I moved one of the bigger chunks around in my hand, I saw a smooth straight hole that looked like it had been bored through it.

“Hey, look at this.“ I held it up for Justine.

“That could be from a tie or nail or anything. I think you’re grasping for something that’s not there.”

“If it were a nail, there would be rust stains. The ties are metal, too; you would see some kind of evidence. ” I brought the piece to an adjacent table that had a lighted magnifying lens mounted to it and studied the hole. There were grooves on the side walls, as if a drill bit had made them. I hesitated to submit my findings to Justine's cynical review. There could be any number of reasons for a hole to be bored into the concrete. Burkett's earlier search of the barge told me he'd been looking for something. Not knowing exactly where the sample had come from made it difficult to dismiss it.

"Whatcha got there?" Justine came over to look.

"Looks like something bored this," I said, enjoying the closeness as we pressed our faces together to look.

"Interesting." She walked away.

I wasn't sure if she had spoken sarcastically, but when she returned with a tool that looked like a scalpel and a collection tray, I started to think I might have found something significant. She took the piece from me and carefully scraped a sample of the concrete from the area surrounding the hole.

"You see the discoloration? That doesn't match

any of the other colors."

I'd been so focused on the hole that I hadn't looked around it. Concrete might appear grey when it is finished because the water, or cream as it is known in the trade, forced to the outside by either vibration or a finishing tool, is mostly Portland cement. In this case there'd be a combination of cement and fly ash. Inside, however, the aggregate or small rocks have unique and natural color. Looking at the area of the sample I realized that the discoloration wasn't natural. Just as I realized what it was, Justine confirmed it.

"This is some kind of residue from a blast. I'm going to run some tests."

I wasn't sure which way I wanted this to go. If she was correct, it would be the difference between faulty construction and sabotage which, since six people were killed, would be the difference between manslaughter and murder. I walked over to the table where Justine was working and watched her as she placed the sample under a microscope. While she focused the lenses using the binocular viewfinder, I watched on the computer monitor. My untrained eyes detected nothing, but when Justine looked up, I could tell from her smile that we had found something.

"These spherical pieces shouldn't be here," she said, pointing to a spot on the monitor.

The image on the screen looked like a meteor shower from a science fiction movie. "Can you tell what they are?"

"Not without running further tests. Maybe this should wait until later when I have the place to myself."

I agreed. "I've had no luck delaying the ceremony."

"They want this to go away."

That gave me an idea. If I could figure out who the *they* were, I could backtrack to find out who did this. Now that there was evidence of foul play there was only a short list of people who had access. Martinez wanted the ceremony to move forward for his own aggrandizement; though selfish, I knew his motives were just that. The powers that be in Miami-Dade and FIU wanted it off the news and neither had the kind of access required to sabotage the structure. That left the engineer and contractor. With Roslyn pointing her finger at Burkett without a solid case against him, it looked as if she and the engineering firm had the most dubious reason for the bridge to become a reef.

"I think I need to call Grace." It was more thinking out loud and I should have known better. There was some kind of friction between Justine and the detective, but she was one of my only allies here.

"The tampering and failure happened in Miami-Dade's jurisdiction; you probably ought to."

Her reaction surprised me and confirmed that it was the right thing to do. If I could get Grace to buy into my theory it would legitimize the case. "You don't mind, then?" It was a stupid question. Justine was a pro and she rolled her eyes as a response.

"Go ahead. I heard she's got a new partner, too. Your buddy Dick Tracy got a promotion after helping take down the crooked FBI agent."

That was good news for me, but not the department. Tracy was an ex-FBI agent with a grudge. Along with the majority of the police here, he had been wary whenever I was involved. I knew it wasn't personal—but it felt that way. I put my ego aside and found Grace Herrera's contact info on my phone. Composing my argument in my head while it rang, I waited for her to answer.

"Agent Hunter. Long time."

With Justine standing next to me I was glad Grace wasn't one for small talk. "Have you been following the bridge collapse?"

"Not really on our radar. Looks like the contractor screwed up, but it's not criminal."

"Not yet anyway. Are you anywhere near the

crime lab?"

"You going to ruin my night?"

"Maybe."

Chapter 13

While I waited for Grace, Justine went to her workstation to check her messages. I took a minute to text Allie and catch up on my emails. I was worried about my daughter and wanted to see her. If Jane would allow it, having her join me at the ceremony might be both cool and give Allie some closure by watching the bridge debris become a reef.

"I'm going to ask Allie if she can come down to see the ceremony. You interested?" I asked Justine.

"That's a good idea. Might as well join them if we can't stop them. Might be good for her."

I got an enthusiastic emoji from Allie and waited while she asked her mother. A few minutes later, she answered that her mom had said yes. It was no surprise when the phone rang a minute later and

Jane's name showed on the screen.

"Hi," I answered tentatively. "I can run up there and pick her up." If she was going to allow an unscheduled visit I wanted to make it as easy as I could.

"I know you're trying to do the right thing, but once again you set me up to be the bad guy."

Honestly I hadn't thought about putting her in a position that made her the bad parent if she said no. "I'm sorry. Next time I'll ask you first."

"I'm only borderline okay with this. She's been obsessed with the collapse since she got home. Maybe this will give her some closure."

It always stung when she called her house *home*, but I knew that Allie needed a stable place to live while she went to school. "Is she okay?"

"I think she's got your curiosity gene. I just wish she'd use it for school."

"I can be there in a half hour," I said, hoping that would end the conversation.

"Let me make this clear."

I heard the sound of a door closing in the background and braced myself.

"Do not put her in harm's way. I know this was an accident, but you have a knack for finding trouble."

I understood her threat and mentally checked my bank account balance in case I needed the services of my attorney, Daniel J. Viscount. Though it had cost in the five figures, he had done what no other lawyer could and gotten me visitation with Allie. I did not want to have to employ his services again and promised Jane I would do my best.

She sighed. "I know you mean well, but… "

The lab was generally like a library. The only sounds were muted conversations and machine noises from the equipment. A loud voice broke the silence and caught my attention. I told Jane I had to go and turned to the entrance, where I saw a man coming toward us. Grace was behind him, saying something that I couldn't make out and when he tried to hug Justine, my first reaction was that I would have preferred Dick Tracy. This didn't look like the start of a good relationship.

"You must be Hunter," the man said, extending his hand. "John Traynor, but everyone calls me JT."

I wondered if he had given himself the nickname. JT stood a full six inches below me. His combover was ineffective at hiding his bald spot and his greasy hair only accentuated the rumpled look, complete with a three-day beard that was patchy at best. Without even knowing him, I felt sorry for Grace.

Detective Herrera was a knockout. Carefully groomed and standing just two inches shy of my six feet, she was fit and trim. Side by side these two looked like the Odd Couple.

"What do you have for us, Hunter? I've heard you're not scared to waste our resources." He spoke with a slight accent that I couldn't place.

I turned to Grace. "Justine can show you what we found, then I'll brief you."

Justine smiled. She always enjoyed a bit of what my grandfather called *shadenfreuder*, guilty pleasure at another's misfortune. She was clearly enjoying Grace's bad luck. I was more in the "enemy of my enemy is my friend" camp. If it took her rumpled partner to give the women a common antagonist that put them on better terms, he was my friend.

"Where're you from? I can't place the accent," I asked JT while Justine explained to Grace the evidence revealed by the microscope. He ignored my attempt to befriend him.

"Some detective you are," he said.

Grace saved me from any further conversation. "So, you think this is a murder now?"

I started to explain what I had learned about concrete, until I noticed both their eyes had begun to wander. Justine's look told me to get on with it. "The engineer's done a pretty good job at throwing the contractor under the bus."

"And your point is?" JT asked, waving his hands as if to dismiss my argument.

I needed to get them to buy in so I tried a different tack. "Why would he blow up his own bridge? Don't think he's going to get paid now."

"Maybe he's not too bright. He is a contractor. "

I could feel the blood rush to my face and tried to control it. JT was not going to be won over. I turned to Grace. "I've met the guy several times. We saw him yesterday, when we caught him out on the barge searching the debris for something."

"Or burying it," JT said.

"It's going to get buried at 9:00 tomorrow morning. Why interfere if that's his goal?"

"Okay, kids," Justine interrupted. "The forensics tech says that someone tried to sabotage the bridge. It resulted in the death of six innocent people. How about we play nicely together and try and solve this?"

"You're sure the evidence is conclusive?" Grace

asked her.

"You can possibly explain the bore hole, but not the residue from the explosion."

"Okay, Hunter," she finally agreed. "I'll kick it upstairs and see what they want to do." Grace motioned to her partner and they walked away. I could hear him yammering until they were out the door.

It was the best that I could hope for. After the last few cases, my picture was probably on the wall in every breakroom in Dade County. At this point, anything that had my name attached to it would have to be approved. I could only hope it was Grace doing the explaining and not JT.

I turned to Justine. "I'm going to pick up Allie. Want to get a bite to eat when we get back?"

"That'd be cool. I'll see if I can get a chemical breakdown on this by then."

I glanced around the now empty lab and, seeing only a few lights, I leaned in and pecked her on the cheek. She punched my arm in return, letting me know we were all good.

I checked my watch before I left and saw I was already five minutes late. After texting Jane, I left the lab and headed to the truck. In a hurry, I hit the bar on the entry door and pushed it open, only to find I had slammed it into James Burkett. He fell to his knees. It was like déjà vu from the other night.

"Agent Hunter, any luck?" His speech was noticeably slurred.

I flinched when I grabbed him under the arms to help him up. The smell of alcohol was strong, and looking into his bloodshot eyes I knew I couldn't leave him here. "Come on. I have to run an errand. We can talk on the way."

I was hoping for a couple of outcomes. First that with the alcohol in his system his guard would be down enough that when I told him about what we had found that I could get a genuine reaction out of him. The second was that he didn't drive himself anywhere. There was a third thing that should have been at the front of my mind, and that was that Jane didn't see him.

After helping him into the back seat of the truck, I went around and got in the driver's side. He started mumbling something that I ignored until we were on the highway.

"Any idea why there are holes bored in the concrete and residue of an explosive around them?" I looked ahead with one eye and adjusted the rearview mirror to see his face with the other. He was slouched in the seat with his head down, making it hard to read his expression, but something told me he didn't know anything about it.

"Why?" he asked. "She knows this will ruin me."

He cradled his head in his hands and I turned all my attention to the road ahead. "I don't know. You think this was aimed at you personally?"

"I didn't mean it like that. I know people died. But…"

Whatever he was about to say was lost when I saw we'd almost passed the exit. As I slammed on the brakes, I was grateful Allie wasn't with me. With my tires screeching and my full concentration on the road ahead, I turned toward the exit lane and pulled off the highway. Careful to stay inside the shoulder, I backed up and pulled onto the exit ramp. Jane's house was just a few blocks away so our discussion would have to wait…which was probably for the better. His inebriated state had shown me the truth: he was not involved. Now, I needed to prep him and hope that he comprehended.

"I'm picking up my daughter. Can you just stay down when we get there until I tell you it's okay to sit back up?" I asked, hoping that he could control his actions.

"Ex-wife, I'm guessing. Been there; done that—three times. I get it, Hunter."

His speech was slurred, but I thought he understood. I could only hope so as I pulled to the curb in front of the 1960s ranch house. In another area, the small lots and older houses would have been a warning sign that this was not a neighborhood where I would want my daughter to grow up. But here, the houses and yards were well-maintained, and several of the older houses had been torn down to make room for new construction. Less than a mile from The Intercoastal Waterway, the old neighborhood was a desirable location.

I pulled up at the curb and saw the exterior lights come on. Being proactive in the hope that Jane wouldn't see Burkett, I got out and went to the door.

"Hey, Dad," Allie burst past me and headed to the truck.

"You going to say good-bye?" I called after her, not wanting her to see Burkett before I could lay some groundwork. She turned back and with her head down, dragging her feet like it hurt to walk, she said a dramatic good-bye and hugged Jane. I got a smile from my ex for my efforts and said good night, hoping there was still a chance to get out of here before Burkett showed himself.

We were almost to the truck when I saw the interior light come on and then heard a loud hacking cough. I cleared my throat, trying to make it sound like it had come from me, but the timing just wasn't there.

"Kurt, someone you want to introduce us to?"

I grasped for the right words. "Just doing a friend a favor."

"Is this *friend* someone that Allie needs to know?"

Allie saw her opportunity to attend the ceremony being torn from her by her dad's bad decisions. She was not to be deterred and went to the truck.

"It's just Ray, Mom. You know, the guy that lives out on the island with Dad."

I shrugged, not wanting to admit to myself that if she could lie this easily, what might I be missing?

Jane must have bought it because she turned away. I wasted no time and picked up Allie's bag. I started to toss it into the back seat, but judging from the way Burkett had folded himself into the seat. I decided it would be better in the bed.

Allie allowed me a few minutes to get out of sight of the house before the interrogation began. I answered the "who is he and what is he doing here" part. She found it amusing that he was drunk and wanted to know what he had drunk and how much. After hearing her lie so easily and now witnessing her fascination with my drunken new friend, I realized that she was growing up faster than I wanted to admit.

Chapter 14

Burkett passed out as soon as we hit the highway, giving me a chance to explain to Allie why he was here. I stopped short of thanking her for lying. As much as I appreciated her bailing me out, I couldn't support bad behavior. It's hard enough to figure out what reaches your kids; what they need to be taught and what they already know. I could only hope she realized she had crossed a line.

We reached the crime lab and Allie's curiosity moved from drunks and alcohol to Justine. I hadn't planned on going inside, but she insisted. Since Burkett was still sound asleep in the back seat I decided to leave him where he was. There were still several reporters hanging around and the last thing he needed was to be interviewed and photographed in his present state.

Justine met us at the security door to the lab and after she and Allie embraced they headed off together for a quick tour. My stomach was grumbling, but watching the two of them together took the edge off. I sat down with my phone to see what I had missed in the past hour, especially whether Grace had had any luck with the Ivory Tower.

The message screen was blank and there was nothing important in my emails. I decided to be proactive and started composing a note to Martinez to let him know that Justine and Allie would be with me tomorrow. I figured if I sent it late enough he wouldn't read it until after the ceremony anyway; the email was kind of like asking for forgiveness instead of permission.

By the time Justine and Allie returned I was having trouble keeping my eyes open. We left the lab and went back to the truck. Burkett was still sleeping in the back seat. Now I had to decide what to do with him. Tossing him to the curb was not an option, nor was letting him drive. I opened the door and shook him. I figured if I could wake him, I might get an address that I could send him to in an Uber, but he only mumbled gibberish at me.

"What's he doing back there?" Justine asked.

I explained about finding him, leaving out the part about his performance at Jane's house, or Allie's lie. "I'll ride back there; you can drive." I handed the keys to Justine.

"I can drive," Allie said.

I looked over at him and wondered about the ethics of using Burkett for an excuse. I decided to go with it. "I can't with him in back."

Allie seemed to buy it and got into the passenger seat. Justine drove us to one of our favorites, a Thai restaurant that had pretty good food and excellent hours; they would still be open. Burkett was still out when we reached the parking lot, and I left him in the back seat.

Though I had no logical reason for it, I still felt a twinge of apprehension whenever Justine and Allie were together. I knew I had nothing to worry about, but the chance that one might say the wrong thing and put me in a bind lurked below the surface. Thankfully, the feeling usually wore off quickly.

Tonight was different, though; probably because I was having a hard time staying present in the conversation. My phone lay face up on the table in front of me and between staring at it with the hope that Grace would call, and my obsession with the case, I heard little of what was being said. I caught a few glances from Justine, but she must have understood, and the two gladly chatted through dinner as if I wasn't there.

"What are you going to do with the boy wonder? You can't take him back to your house," Justine said when we were leaving.

"I know. I'll try and wake him up and put him in an Uber." I went to the truck and shook him. Slowly his eyes opened, then I had to settle him down when he realized he didn't know where he was. It took a few minutes for him to join the living, but he seemed surprisingly sober. It had been two hours since I had found him and the effects of the alcohol had mostly worn off. I thought about taking him back to his car and letting him go, but Justine put a stop to that.

"You let him drive and he gets pulled over, it's on you. There's probably still enough alcohol in his system for a DUI."

I looked over at Allie, who was watching with morbid fascination, and I knew that whatever I decided to do now would influence her future decisions. Justine was right. After getting an address from him, I ordered an Uber.

"You need to get his keys. He could talk the driver into taking him back to his car instead of driving him home," Justine said.

She was right again, and I looked back at Burkett. His head had fallen back and he started to snore. My patience with babysitting him was gone and I reached into his pocket for his keys. My hand found a key ring with several keys, along with something else that I couldn't identify.

"Let me see that," Justine said.

Just as she and Allie leaned in to see what I had found, the Uber arrived. I put the small cylinder in my pocket and loaded Burkett into the backseat of a fairly clean Corolla. Figuring a little damage control wouldn't hurt, I removed the truck key from his keychain and handed the driver the remaining keys with a twenty as a tip in case Burkett lost his lunch in the man's car.

None of this fazed the driver and he pocketed the cash with a quick thank you. After checking on Burkett again, I pulled the cylinder out of my pocket and handed it to Justine. I thought I knew what it was and she confirmed it.

"A blasting cap. How cool," Allie said. "Can I see it?"

"It's evidence," I said, reaching into the glove compartment and pulling out a bag. Even though I had grabbed it from his pocket, I used the tips of my fingers now as I placed it in the bag and sealed it.

"Did that have something to do with the bridge?" Allie asked.

I wasn't sure what to tell her and decided on the truth. She seemed equally as fascinated with the crime lab as she had been with Burkett's binge. I looked at Justine for help.

"We can take it back to the lab and examine it," she said.

"Really? Can I help?" Allie asked.

Justine had already drifted into work mode and didn't answer. "We'll see," I said, giving her a standard dad response.

When we reached the lab the lot was empty. I guessed the reporters had called it a day after the deadline for the 11:00 news and the morning papers had expired. We entered the lab and Justine went to her workstation, where she placed the evidence bag on the table.

"Have to get the concrete samples," she said, and went to the *vault*, her name for the evidence room. Unlike the old locker, the new one had thick smoked glass doors and LED lights that gave it an eerie look. Justine entered her code in the keypad and the doors opened with a *swoosh.* The effect of the negative pressure in the room gave the impression that a seal had been broken. She emerged a minute later with a box and brought it back to the table.

"Here we go," she said as she opened the lid and removed the samples we had taken from the barge.

With the concrete sample secured in a vise, she held the cylinder with a pair of tweezers. With Allie and I leaning in to watch she slowly lay the metal piece onto the groove. It sat perfectly. There was no question that the hole had been bored for the cylinder.

"Now that we know what went in the hole, let's

see if we can't figure out what it is."

"It's a blasting cap." I had seen many like it in the Plumas forest. Despite a hundred and fifty years of mining, the streams there still held gold. Over the years regulations had limited mining in California, reducing it from large-scale operations involving acres of land and heavy equipment, to small dredging operations. Many of the miners worked on legal claims, but I had run across many illegal operations. It was hard, slow work, and many miners cut corners by blasting the larger boulders to access the alluvial deposits possibly hidden underneath them.

"Right, Special Agent, but if you want to find out who did it, we need to find out what kind of detonator was used. There are electrical, chemical, mechanical, and all kinds of hand-made ones out there. Check it out on YouTube."

Allie immediately pulled out her phone. I glanced over at her and she put it back in her pocket, but I guessed she would be searching later. "Okay, but it looks like Burkett has blood on his hands."

We followed her to another area of the lab. First Justine removed whatever fingerprints and residue were on the cylinder, then she started to dissect it. I saw the wires and knew immediately that it had been remotely detonated. Justine quickly confirmed my guess and we stood around the table staring at the parts lying there.

"The detonator probably disintegrated in the blast," I said.

"Parts of it may still be on the barge. If they dump it, the evidence will be lost."

I had no expectations that something the size of a deck of cards sitting next to the explosion would be recoverable. But there was always a chance; what I did know was that the material was going to be sitting under sixty feet of water in less than twelve hours.

"We need to go out there tonight," I said.

"Really?" Allie asked.

There was no leaving her out of this, and

another set of eyes could only help. I did a ten-second risk analysis in my head and determined that this fell into the Adventure Category with Minimal Risk. I would of course swear her to secrecy, but the wind had died down from this morning and I didn't think safety was going to be a concern.

"Okay." I looked at Justine.

"Onward, Kimo sabe," she said, and started packing up the evidence.

Once she had placed it back in the *vault*, we left the lab and headed to the truck. I could tell by the way that Allie was rambling on about anything and everything that she was excited. Justine had that look in her eye as well. I didn't share their optimism, and as I drove south on the Turnpike another thought started nagging at me.

If the bridge failure had not been the result of overtightened tension bolts as the engineer claimed, or of faulty concrete as Burkett was so adamant about, then the collapse had been a premeditated act.

There would be a motive, and I also wondered how the timing of the blast had been determined.

If the purpose of the failure had been to demonstrate that fly ash couldn't replace Portland cement, or that a bolt was too tight, then why not blow the thing up in the middle of the night when no one was around?

Instead, the failure had occurred during a moderately busy time of day. Whoever had detonated the explosion had to have known there would be collateral damage. I continued down this train of thought until I realized the detonation might have been timed to kill someone in particular.

Chapter 15

Now came the question of how much I wanted to involve Allie. She was in, so far as we were already headed to the reef site to look for physical evidence before it was dropped to the sea floor. I wanted to follow up on my new theory, but decided against including her, at least until I could confirm it. Searching through a pile of concrete and steel was not the same thing as speculating on whether one of the victims of the catastrophe actually had been a target.

For our purposes tonight, it didn't really matter.

Spray flew off the low bow of the boat, giving us a misting that brought me back to the present. The wind had dropped, but the seas were still running about two feet, only slightly less than this morning. The bay waters at night were something that needed to be respected. Depending on the season, outside of the park boundaries lobster and crab buoys could be a minefield to nighttime boaters. Inside the boundaries it was generally safe, unless you hit a piece of debris. There were many hazards in the shallow bay waters, most well-marked with lights. Even without a chart plotter, as long as you remembered the three R's—right, red, return—and kept the red markers or lights to starboard when inbound, you would be safe.

I dropped the RPMs and let the engine settle before raising the tilt of the engine slightly until the boat started to porpoise, then dropped it down slightly until it leveled out. Once I found the correct trim, I steered through the channel at the Featherbed Bank and headed for the open water to the north of Boca Chita Key. The lighthouse there was ornamental and had no functioning light of its own, but the security lights scattered around the campground gave the same information.

Once we were clear of Boca Chita there were no more barrier islands to slow down the surge of the open Atlantic waters and I had to readjust the trim and drop speed again. This time I caught it before taking on any water. On the way out I'd been worried about finding the site at night, but the barge was lit by security lights now. They weren't from the barge itself, but from another, larger barge with a crane tied up next to it. A large ship was also stationed nearby. I could tell right away from its position that it was anchored and assumed from its size that it was a Coast Guard Cutter.

Without saying a word, I aborted our mission and spun the wheel to reverse course. Justine and Allie had come to the same conclusion, and we all glanced back, wondering if we had been seen. It was my park, but a nighttime confrontation with the Coasties was not good for anyone—you were assumed guilty until you proved your innocence. Without a light bar on the park service boat, we would not be recognized until they were within gunshot range. A radio call might buy us some time, but we would be under observation, something that wouldn't serve my purpose of being here.

Once we were in the lee of Boca Chita Key, I slowed.

"No way we can go crawl around that wreckage tonight. The large ship was likely a Coast Guard Cutter and there's no telling who else is lurking out there."

"I saw some white lights nearby," Allie said.

Her young eyes had done well. "There's probably going to be quite a crowd tomorrow; those are probably folks staking out their spots." Martinez might have been right in assigning me a sector to patrol. I hadn't thought this was going to be a big deal, but from the boats already out it looked like I was wrong. "I guess we head back home and get an early start tomorrow."

They agreed and I pushed down the throttle for

the ride back to Adams Key. Staying to the inside and under the protection of the barrier islands, the seas were flat and we reached the dock twenty minutes later. With Justine at the bow and Allie at the stern, we docked and froze, waiting for the inevitable.

We had tried to be quiet, but Zero's radar must have alerted him that Allie and Justine were with me. For a brief second I thought we had gotten away with it, but then I heard the screen door slam and after a slight delay—when he descended the stairs from the stilt house—all fifty pounds of him came bowling toward us.

Allie and Justine fell for his act and gave him the attention he felt he deserved.

"Hunter, is that you?" Ray called down from the deck.

"Yeah, sorry about that. We tried to get in without waking him."

"Got the women with you. He knows. Can't sleep anyhow, bunch of fools come by trying to camp here earlier, thinking they could see that pile of concrete get dumped. What the hell is with these people?"

It took several attempts for him to get Zero's attention, but finally, knowing where his food bowl was, the big dog strolled back upstairs. The door slammed again and we had a quiet laugh. I checked that the boat was secure and followed Allie and Justine up to the house.

It had been awkward at first with both of them staying here. On the second weekend with me sleeping on the couch, Allie had asked me when I was going to marry her. I didn't want to tell her that I hadn't even told her I loved her yet, but her question had given me permission to cohabitate. After deciding on a six a.m. start, we said good night and went to bed.

I lay awake for what felt like hours, until Justine finally turned on the light and asked me what was wrong. After explaining my theory that this might have been a targeted killing, she rolled out of bed and grabbed my laptop.

"Should be pretty easy to see who the victims were," she said as she started typing something into the Google search bar.

I waited, feeling guilty that I was causing both of us to lose sleep. "Sorry about this. I can sleep on the couch."

"No worries. Your problems are my problems."

I liked the sound of that and reached for her. She brushed off my advances and focused on the screen.

"Here you go. Guess we'll have to do a search for each one. I don't recognize any of the names." She swung the screen so I could see it.

"Wait, I recognize that name."

It looked familiar, but I couldn't place it. She gave me the *I'm waiting* look and I shrugged. After Justine entered the name into Google again, I moved closer and we looked at the results together. There were Facebook and LinkedIn profiles that we clicked through, but still nothing. "Maybe I'm just tired. Let's look at the other names."

One at a time we performed the same search on each of the victims. They all seemed like ordinary people to me.

"Why would someone go through all that trouble?" Justine asked.

"Money, power, greed, you know the deal. But none of the victims appears related to anything that has to do with the bridge." My eyes were heavy and I caught Justine nodding off. The laptop was by my side now and I looked over at Justine. She had fallen asleep sitting up. I stowed the computer under the bed and eased her into a more comfortable position before turning off the light and calling it a night, hoping sleep would finally take me.

It apparently did, because a knock on the door woke both of us. The first rays of light were streaming through the blinds as I reached for my phone. It was already six. and we were supposed to be on the water. I called out to Allie that we would be ready in a few minutes and woke Justine.

The day couldn't have been any better if Martinez had requisitioned it. Somehow his media Karma was holding up and the swell that we had felt last night was gone. By the time we were ready to go the seas were flat and the sun was already out. I expected the usual round of afternoon thunderstorms, but the ceremony would be finished before the small puffy clouds had time to turn into the mean anvil-shaped thunderheads that kept you vigilant about the weather this time of year.

We quickly packed a cooler with some food and drinks and headed out the door. Ray and Becky were loading their boat for a picnic as well. We were delayed slightly when Zero, now stuck on Ray's boat, had a fit of jealousy when Allie went to say hi to Jamie.

"Y'all gonna go catch the show too? Don't think

it'll be as good as when they scuttle a boat to make a wreck site, but it's still pretty cool," Becky said.

"Gotta work an area, but I'm hoping we can see it," I told her.

"This weather, there ought to be a whole lot of yahoos out there," Ray said. "We're going to head to the beach at Boca Chita after if you want to join us."

I thanked him for the invitation and started the engine. Ray left the dock ahead of us and I waited to see if he was going to take the inside or outside route before releasing the lines. His boat had just disappeared through Caesar Creek when I turned the other way. Ray liked to run fast and had taken the open water route. I chose the inside, both to have two sets of eyes on the water and to satisfy Martinez if he happened to be watching.

We were far from the first boats on the water. An overhead shot from one of the news helicopters circling overhead would have shown three lines of boats all heading to the site: Bayfront and Blackpoint

Parks from the south and Government Cut from the north.

The park service boat was nondescript. With just the forest green T-top and logo on the sides, most boaters probably thought we were just another group heading out. It was going to be a party-like atmosphere and I was thankful that the early hour had probably kept the alcohol consumption down—at least for now. Later, with all the packed boats, with equally packed coolers, there were bound to be some issues.

A traffic jam had formed at the cut through the Featherbed Banks and I slowed to advise several impatient boaters where the shallows were. We stuck around there longer than I would have liked, directing the traffic to go single-file through the channel. Finally, rush hour ended and I jumped in behind a large cruiser playing loud rap music.

Martinez wanted me on the inside of the site and I took up a station about a hundred yards from the barge. Allie took the binoculars from the console and scanned the horizon. It was almost nine and the show was about to start.

"Hey, there's your boss." Allie pointed to the Coast Guard Cutter we had seen last night.

I reached for the binoculars and focused on the deck. There he was in his finest dress uniform. Susan McLeash was at his side, and I wondered what she had done to get out of her patrol. It didn't matter, really; she and the rest of the crowd were probably safer with her surrounded by the Coast Guard.

A loud boom sounded and the crane that had stationed itself next to the barge reached down and scooped up the first piece of debris. Cheers went up from the crowd, but we were quiet as we watched the evidence drop to the sea floor.

Chapter 16

Twenty minutes later it was over. The tugs that had been stationed off to the side were reunited with the barges and started to tow them back to port. Spectators stayed for a few minutes, then started to drift away. The helicopters made one more pass before heading back to Miami. A few minutes later, the Coast Guard vessel pulled anchor and moved off. We were alone except for a lone red buoy marking the site.

I idled close to the site of the new reef. Later this week, eighteen white mooring balls would be added to allow recreational divers access to the site without having to anchor. We reached the buoy and peered over the side. The flat seas and clear water showed little of the collapsed bridge—just some dark patches on the otherwise sandy bottom.

"We have a small window here before it's swarmed with divers and fishermen." I had heard that newly placed reefs were prime attractions for both recreational and commercial dive boats. The history of the reef, as well as the convenience of the mooring buoys, would make it hard to pass up. Most of the other artificial reefs in the park were wrecks in various states of decay, like the one we had dove on last weekend. The bridge, although not as interesting a dive, held a morbid fascination about it. It would be a busy site.

"What do you mean?" Allie asked.

I started to backtrack. Diving the bridge wreckage now would give us our last opportunity to see if there was any evidence. Finding anything would be a slim chance, but sometimes you had to take what you were given. By the weekend, the site would be dotted with mooring buoys. Even before that, the beginnings of a slime coat would form, one that would eventually hide the concrete entirely. Colonies of coral and other life would then begin to establish themselves.

My only issue with diving it so soon was that I wasn't sure if the concrete chunks were likely to shift as they settled into their final resting place, making the dive dangerous. I thought myself barely qualified to dive the site this soon after being dumped; there was no way I was going to endanger Allie.

"We should plan on diving it next weekend," I decided. It would be marked, but everyone else would be searching for lobster. I doubted after only a week that the site would hold many of the highly sought after crustaceans. It was also sportsman's season and with only two days, hunters tended to go to spots they knew and leave exploration of new areas for later in the season.

"That sounds great, Dad," Allie said, turning back to her phone.

She sat on the padded cooler top in front of the console, posting pictures she'd taken of the reef being sunk on Facebook and Instagram. Justine came close to me.

"Next weekend will be too late," she whispered.

"I know, but it's too dangerous for Allie."

As we pulled away from the site, a part of my brain started a countdown. Every minute the rubble was in the water the chances of finding any other evidence grew slimmer. "You're part of the Miami-Dade dive team, right?" I asked Justine. Between the background noise from the idling engine and her position in front of the console and windshield, I didn't think Allie could hear us as long as we spoke quietly.

"Roger that, Kimo sabe. I'll send a group text and see if anyone is interested."

I would have to figure out how to get myself invited later, but even if I was excluded at least I would have eyes down there. "You can use the park service boat. I'll run you out."

"That might help," she said.

That would also keep me close. "Ready?" I yelled over the console to Allie. I waited until she'd stashed her phone to press down on the throttle. We were quickly up on plane speeding back to Adams Key.

Despite the ticking clock in my head and the nagging feeling that there was something I was missing, the beauty of the park quickly captivated me. The subtle pastels of the crystal clear water spread in front of me. The colors held clues to the bottom features but were so beautiful on their own that thousands of artists had tried to replicate them—most falling short. White ibis and pelicans crowded the mangrove-lined shores and mullet jumped in the small coves.

Elliot Key was on our port side and Adams Key, our destination, lay dead ahead. I slowed slightly, realizing that once we reached the key, I had no plan. Martinez would expect a report from me, but I figured the media coverage would keep him occupied for the rest of the day. A larger fish left the water in chase of some invisible prey to our right and Allie called out to see if we had seen it.

Fishing had a way of solving my problems. Maybe it was the absolute focus of the hunt or just being immersed in nature that made my brain work differently. Either way, the single-minded pursuit was the secret sauce. Whenever I called it quits and put away the rod and reel, my mind had usually worked through my problems. That's when things usually came together for me.

"We've got some time. Want to chase a few fish?" I got a unanimous thumbs-up. "Okay, we'll stop by the dock and grab some poles. Jones Lagoon should be pretty good on this tide." It had taken me some time to become one with the ebb and flow of the tides and currents here, but I rarely needed to check the tide tables anymore.

An hour later I dropped the Power-Pole that secured the boat in the shallow lagoon. Without a marked channel leading through the maze of mangroves, it was almost always quiet in here. We started casting swim baits under the branches and I smiled when Allie hooked up first. Even her disappointment when the fish broke off in the tangled roots resulted in a determined smile.

Pretty soon we were all landing small snapper. It was fun, especially watching Allie—she was still new enough at this that any tug on the other end of the line was exciting. She hadn't yet been ruined by that one good day when you loaded the boat with keepers. Justine held her own, and I spent more time unhooking and tossing fish back than fishing. It was all good, but gave me little time to think about the case.

We stayed with it until the tide bottomed out and the bite slowed. After stowing the rods, I went to raise the Power-Pole and head back when the sound of my phone ringing broke the silence. I should have known my reprieve from Martinez would be short-lived. The ceremony was over and the bridge debris was underwater. His appearance had already been shown live and was now on tape ready for the evening news. I'm sure he already knew which bar his most influential friends would be drinking at later so he could join them and make sure they saw him prominently featured in the coverage. Until then it was business as usual.

"Hunter, I'm guessing you're patrolling in there," he started.

Of course he knew where I was from the tracker on the boat and my phone. "Somebody's got to do it."

"Now that the reef is in place, you need to submit a schedule and stop this wild goose chase. This investigation or whatever you're doing is over."

I paused for a second before answering. There was no way I was going to give in and drop the case, especially after finding the bored hole and blasting cap. I started feeling guilty that I had taken the last hour to fish. "I'll be back at headquarters in an hour."

That bought me a little time to figure out what I was going to do. Going to see him was on my route to take Justine and Allie back anyway. Justine had to work later and especially after Jane had seen Burkett last night, I wanted to get Allie back as promised. "Let's head back. It's getting to be about that time."

I idled out of the lagoon and entered the deep-water channel that dead-ended there. One of the many remnants of attempts to develop the out islands, there were many of these partially marked channels that ended abruptly. Minutes later, Zero greeted us as we docked. Allie and Justine went up to the house to clean up and grab their things while I put away the fishing gear.

It sometimes felt like I had two lives: one with Allie and Justine when we were like a close-knit family, the other as a loner. The closer we all became the less I liked the latter.

Ray must have seen us come in and came down the steps from his house. "Fishing any good?" he asked.

"Fair. Bunch of small stuff. Nothing for the pan."

"Martinez wants to get the mooring balls set before the weekend. If you don't have much on your plate, I could use a hand."

These kind of duties usually fell to Ray. When you wanted to get something done here, he was the man. "I'm going in to see him now. I'll ask." If he went for it, the assignment would allow me access to the new reef and also get Martinez off my back for a few days. Both worked with my agenda.

The second the screen door to my house closed, Zero went on full alert. He glanced over at me and ran up the path, where he waited at the bottom of the stairs for Allie and Justine. They stopped to pet him and he followed them to the dock, clearly upset when we untied the lines and pulled away.

It was a beautiful summer day that didn't yet hold the threat of thunderstorms. Between the weather and the ceremony this morning, there was still a lot of traffic on the water, enough that the white water from the wakes of boats going in both directions looked like the markings on a highway. I waited for a space and merged into the side that was heading back to the ramp at Bayfront Park. I wasn't sure I was happy about the additional traffic, but I knew Martinez would see it as a boon for his budget, which would make my request a slam dunk.

It was no surprise to see Susan's boat tied up in its slip, and I backed into mine, hoping that I could get Martinez alone. She would find some reason to object to my request just because it was my request. After I secured the boat, Justine and Allie went to the truck while I went inside.

Mariposa confirmed that Martinez was still in a good mood, and after hearing that Allie and Justine were outside waiting, she decided to take her break and went to see them. Tentatively I walked up the stairs and approached the open door to Martinez's office. Susan was sitting across from him and I clenched my jaw before entering.

"Hunter, we're clear that this is a reef now and not a bridge, right?"

"Yes." That fact was obvious. "There's an awful lot of boat traffic out there. I think we should make it a priority to set the mooring buoys. Ray and I can probably have it done before the weekend."

We all knew that buoys were a huge help in limiting the number of boaters and divers on a particular site. The proper way to anchor was to check the current and position the boat so the anchor was set in the sand and the boat drifted back over the reef. This was lost on many boaters, who dropped anchor directly on the reef and used a short scope to stay above it. Rather than use a retrieval method, many simply pulled the anchor with their engine. The wear and tear on the delicate ecosystem from the jerking of the anchors and chain was harmful to the reef. On every dive I had done that did not have mooring balls, I had seen anchors and chain littering the bottom. On the natural reefs, the balls eliminated the need to anchor, which saved the coral. Chunks of concrete like the bridge debris would also be an anchor magnet, making the mooring balls desirable.

"Right. I'm thinking that Susan can run the regular patrols and you and Ray can set the mooring balls."

I saw the look on Susan's face when she heard this. That was a lot less desk time and a lot more boat time than she was used to. The allocation of resources actually made sense—which made me worry. This was not how we usually rolled around here.

Chapter 17

After dropping off Justine, I headed north on 95 to take Allie home. My worry about Jane seeing Burkett last night turned out to be nothing—because she wasn't there. Now I had a new fear, that Allie would be home alone. I should have known at close to sixteen that she would be by herself sometimes; Jane was thankfully employed which cut down on my payments. The last time we had been a family I would never have left her, but that had been close to two years ago—an eternity in any teenager's life.

I tried to control my emotions while I watched her use her own key to let herself into the house—something else I didn't know. There was no doubt in my mind that it was the right decision to allow her to essentially live here full-time. The stability was good for her. But it hurt that I was missing parts of her growing up. She waved goodbye and the door closed.

I had no other plans and wanted to sit there and keep watch, but I knew she would be upset by my hovering. Slowly I pulled away from the curb and seconds later my phone dinged with a smiley face emoji. I smiled. The right thing isn't always the easiest, but it often pays dividends.

Thinking about doing the right thing, I knew I needed to do something about Burkett. Finding the blasting cap in his pocket implicated him in a way that needed to go through the procedural channel. As much as I felt sorry for the guy, I had to call Grace.

She answered and agreed to meet at her favorite coffee shop. These meetings were sometimes awkward, but it was better than having the eyes of Miami-Dade watching me if I came into the station. Besides, she couldn't get her unpronounceable coffee drink from the drip machine there.

I got there first, ordered a black coffee, and sat

at a corner table. While I waited I pulled out my phone and caught up on my email. I was surprised to find a message from Sid. The nighttime, almost retired, ex-Jersey coroner usually called or texted, but after seeing his message had been sent at four a.m., I silently thanked him for the courtesy. He was probably just getting to work now and I called him back.

"My favorite Ranger. I guess you haven't been fishing lately."

I knew he was referring to my penchant for hooking floaters instead of fish. "Nope, just the usual."

"I was speaking to Detective Herrera yesterday about another matter, and she noticed that I had the bodies from the bridge collapse ahead of me. She said that you had an interest in the incident."

I wondered where this was going, but knew there was no rushing him. "I started on the bodies and found something on one that was a little odd," he said.

Alarm bells were going off in my head and I kicked myself for not reaching out to him first. Autopsies were standard procedure for any unnatural deaths. "Who was it?" There was a pause and I guessed the question threw him off. It should have been *what* was it.

He paused for a minute. "Maybe you can come down to the office?"

I told him it would be my next stop. Grace had come in and was at the counter waiting for her coffee when I hung up. With her extra large cup in hand she sat across from me. I waited until she took a sip and told her about my run-in with Burkett last night as well as finding the blasting cap in his pocket.

"I'm not sure that's admissible evidence. Considering how you found it, even a half-ass defense attorney would have it thrown out."

I would have to fine-tune my procedural game. "It's enough now to bring him into custody. He's running around like a loose cannon."

"No problem there. I'll have him picked up. I'm guessing you want to be there when we question him?"

I thought about that while she drank. Miami-Dade had a reputation for being hard on suspects. I was also the only ally Burkett thought he had. "Maybe a little good cop, bad cop." I explained my plan. "See if he asks for me first."

"Okay. I'll keep you posted." We talked for a minute about her partner situation while she finished her coffee and got up to leave. I got the feeling that she preferred Tracy to her new partner, someone that after meeting him made me wonder about the hiring practices in the Miami-Dade department.

We left the coffee shop together and said good-bye, then headed to our own vehicles. I followed her out of the lot. At the first light, I turned right to head downtown while she went straight in the direction of the station. I caught the mid-afternoon lull in traffic as well as all the lights, making record time to the medical examiner's office.

The building had one of the only basements in Miami, and I shivered as I went down the stairs. In this climate, moisture clung to you and stayed until it fell off or evaporated. The air conditioning felt like a brain freeze to the body as it sucked the moisture from my skin.

I found Sid mumbling to himself while trying to make a cup of coffee at Vance's new machine. The hipster was actually his boss, but that was by agreement and I knew he respected Sid as a senior and mentor. Sid returned that respect except when it came to the stainless steel machine sitting on the counter. I walked over and helped him out.

With his cup in hand, Sid led me into the examination room. I couldn't help but notice when the door closed that over the last year I had become immune to the smell of death. What had once caused me to watch what I ate and made me queasy, now had no effect. One of the victims was laid out on the table, showing the freshly sewn *Y*-shaped incision on his chest.

"Lucky for you, there's nothing on the inside."

Sid reached under the table and grabbed a large plastic bag containing the man's personal effects. I wondered what he was up to. I had expected blood and gore and now it looked like he was handing me a bag of dirty laundry. "Wouldn't this go to the next of kin?"

"Eventually, when we release the body, but you might find something interesting."

I could have gotten angry at him for not just telling me what he knew, but Sid had mentored and nurtured me through my first few bodies here. Out West, I'd had my share of run-ins—all living. Most were meth heads, poachers, and illegal dredgers. I had spent some time at hospitals both getting patched up myself and following up on suspects there, but there had been no dead bodies. Losing my virginity in that area had been made easier by the stooped-over medical examiner.

He was giving me no clue, and I glanced at him. He nodded to a stainless steel table against the sidewall of the room. I put on a pair of gloves, took the bag over, and dumped the contents on the table. There didn't appear to be anything unusual as I sorted through the clothes, underwear, and socks. I moved on to the contents of his pockets, which were in a separate bag inside the larger one. A set of keys, a wallet which I assumed I wasn't the first to pick through and a tube of Chapstick. Not a whole lot to go on. It all lent some perspective to the naked body on the table, but not to my case.

Sid was doing something by the body and I knew better than to ask for his help. Going back to the wallet, I took out my pad and pen to start taking notes. The driver's license told me he was Larry Shelton, a name I recalled from the search Justine and I had done last night. Some quick math told me he was forty-five and the address on his license was in Homestead. Nothing there to raise an alarm. There was a small amount of cash and the usual assortment of credit cards. I recorded the issuing banks and card numbers. In a separate compartment there were about a dozen of his business cards. The logo struck me immediately.

"He worked for the engineering company that designed the bridge."

Sid looked up. "Apparently."

I started to wonder why Roslyn hadn't mentioned this, then quickly recanted. There was no doubt she was devious, but I imagined theirs was a large company. She might not have even known him. I put that in the doubtful-but-possible camp. I took one of the cards, put everything else back in the bag, walked to the autopsy table, and handed it to Sid. He took it and placed it back on the shelf underneath the table.

"Looks like you have some detective work to

do," he said.

"Nothing else unusual?" I asked.

"Not so far. I should be through the rest by morning."

I thanked him and left the subterranean cooler. Walking back outside had the reverse effect as when I had come in and I felt the moisture in the air as it blanketed me. I went back to the truck and once inside opened the window instead of running the air conditioner. I didn't expect the drastic shifts in temperature were good for anyone.

I had my phone in one hand and the card in the other. The more I thought about it there was no way Roslyn hadn't been informed that one of the fatalities had worked for her company. There would have had to be talk about it and plans for a memorial or service. In my years in law enforcement I had learned that coincidences were seldom that. Somehow this man had something to do with the bridge and was killed for it. It would take a cold-blooded calculating killer who knew enough about demolition and bridge construction to cause it to fail right when the man's vehicle was underneath it. The top suspect on that list was hopefully in Miami-Dade's custody by now.

I texted Grace and asked if she had taken Burkett in and when I could speak with him. The answer came back quickly that she had him in custody and I could come down now. He was at the station rather than the county jail, which worked as well. Hopefully while I interviewed Burkett, Grace could run a background check on Larry Shelton.

I hadn't heard from Allie or Justine and texted both a quick *hey*, then headed over to see Burkett. I caught the seven o'clock shift change at the station, doubling the nasty glances I caught on my way upstairs. Grace was behind her desk; her new partner sat in the next cubicle.

"Got a few minutes?" I asked. "I just left Sid and have some information that might be useful."

"Useful to who?" her partner asked.

I ignored him and handed Grace the business card. “Who’s that?”

“One of the victims from the bridge collapse. He works for the same firm that did the engineering.”

“Says here he’s in their testing department.”

“Even more interesting. Maybe he was a whistleblower.” I felt I might have gone too far when her partner rolled back his chair and leaned forward.

“Us real police like to rely on evidence to solve our cases.”

He was becoming increasingly harder to ignore. “Anyway, can we get some information on him?” I handed Grace the page from my pad with his driver’s license and credit card information.

“I’ll have a quick look while you talk to Burkett.” She looked over at her partner.

He got up and led me down the hall to a closed door with a small window glazed with security glass. Removing a key, he opened the door and entered the room. Burkett sat on the right side of a plain table facing what was clearly a one-way mirror. He had a cup of coffee in front of him. "I'll do this myself," I told him.

He gave me a look and relented. "They got recorders and cameras in there," he said, nodding to the mirror.

I was sure they did and he would probably be watching and listening in real time next door. "You okay, James?" I asked, and took the chair across from him.

"You guys have this all wrong. That cap you found, I was going to hand it over to you. Found it at the site. There's no way I would blow up my own bridge."

That was an interesting point. I knew from my dad that good contractors took ownership of their projects. They felt the work was theirs until it was finished, and sometimes afterward. I also knew he hadn't gotten his final payment yet, and now would face a drawn-out court battle to get it.

"You know this guy?" I handed him the business card and watched as the deep red ruts on his face turned white.

Chapter 18

While I waited for Burkett to compose himself, I glanced at the mirror. I knew it was probably standing room only in the small room behind the one-way glass. From his reaction, I half expected the door to be flung open and for us to be surrounded by Miami-Dade officers wearing bulletproof vests and pointing AR-15s at us. He clearly knew something.

"He worked on the project. Did the concrete testing." He thumbed the card.

He was not good at concealing his emotions and I could tell from the look on his face that he was troubled. The problem was that I hadn't told him why I was asking.

I dropped the bomb. "He was killed in the accident."

He looked down and shook his head. Over the years, I've observed the reactions of people when they were given bad news. It was only my opinion, but I believed his reaction now was sincere. I wondered for a second whether the betting line from the spectators behind the glass had changed. What I had to figure out was whether it was because he had just found out the man had died or because he knew he had been discovered.

"Why don't you tell me about him?" I asked, thinking I could draw him out.

"Good guy. A lot of the techs come onto the job site and act like they are real engineers. They make you jump through hoops when they really have little authority. Larry wasn't like that."

I was starting to lean toward the "he-doesn't-know-anything" side. "Was he good at his job?"

"Yeah, concrete testing isn't rocket science. Really just measuring the slump, which is the consistency of the concrete when the material arrives and filling cylinders from each load for testing after it cures."

"So, he didn't make any determinations on site?"

"No, the good testers stay out of the way. I guess their real work is at the lab."

"Anyone have a problem with him?"

"Why would they? He wasn't parading around like that bitch Roslyn or those eco-clowns from FIU. Changing this, that, and the other thing on site. They cost me some money."

But Roslyn was still alive and the tester was dead. After watching Burkett for the past few days, I wasn't sure he could actually kill someone, but if he could, it would more likely have been her. "Any reason someone would want to kill him?"

"You think this is a planned murder—like on TV?"

"You had a blasting cap in your pocket that fit into a hole bored into the concrete. It's too late to tell if that caused the bridge to fail, but the evidence all points in your direction." The only sound that could be heard for the next few minutes was the hum of the ventilation system. I wouldn't go as far as calling it "air conditioning" because the room was bordering on hot—probably some kind of secret police tactic, or the crew next door had turned up the heat for my benefit.

"You have a piece of paper?" he asked.

I left the room for a minute and found Grace and her partner in the hall. "You hear?" We all thought he was ready to write a confession.

"Didn't think you had it in you. They teach you that in Ranger school?" Grace's partner asked.

I wished he had been in a uniform. A name-tag would have helped. Initials ran through my mind: JR, JT. Before I could recall, Grace handed me a legal pad and pen. I took it from her, turned, and took a deep breath before re-entering the room. After handing it to him, I asked Burkett if he wanted a refill of his coffee while he wrote. He took the pad and pen then pushed the cup toward me.

"A little something extra would be nice," he whispered.

I took the cup and left him to write his confession. Word had apparently spread and the aggressive looks I often got from the detectives and officers were tempered—slightly. After refilling the cup, I stopped by Grace's desk. "Anything on the tester?"

"He's clean. Seemed like just an ordinary guy. Graduated from FIU a few years ago and had worked for the engineering company since. No arrests or negative credit."

I thanked her and took the coffee to the interview room. Grace's partner stopped me at the door.

"He's just drawing pictures," he said.

I thought the confession was too good to be true and entered the room without responding. Burkett took the coffee and slid the pad across the table to me. Instead of the expected details of his wrongdoing, there was a sketch of the bridge. Several arrows pointed to what I guessed were critical sections.

"For the size cap that you found to collapse the bridge, there would have had to be several, and the charges would have to be placed at these points." He reached his finger across to emphasize the arrows he had drawn. "There aren't a whole lot of people that would know how to do this—they would have to be involved in the project."

I noticed that his demeanor had changed. The sketch was professionally drawn, especially for the speed with which he had done it. He was now talking like a contractor and not a suspect or victim. Burkett certainly had his problems, but he seemed to be competent at his job.

"Find the material from the adjacent sites and compare the concrete to the cylinders they have. They're supposed to take six from each truck. I know two have probably been crushed for the compressive strength test they do after twenty-eight days. There are two for water permeability tests and they keep two extra. Test them."

He looked spent. This was not the outcome that the room full of Miami-Dade officers probably watching through the one-way mirror wanted, but he seemed sincere and I thought he had done me a favor. I decided to do one in return and turned the pad to a clean page. I scrawled *get a lawyer* on it and slid it across the table. He looked up, relieved, as if he now had a friend, and nodded. After taking the pad back, I tore off the note, stuffed it in my pocket, and left the room.

"What was that all about?" Grace's partner was in my face. He would have been eye to eye if he had another four inches to add to his elevator shoes.

"Sketch of the bridge." I showed him the drawing.

"What's that going to do and what was that note

you wrote?"

"Nothing," I said, inflating my chest and pushing past him. For the police, it was often a worst-case scenario when a suspect lawyered up. I just wanted the truth and if protecting Burkett was going to get it, he deserved an advocate.

I left the building feeling the looks that had been tempered earlier had returned to their previous animosity. On the way to the truck I decided I'd call Grace later and apologize if this had caused her any trouble. For now, I was going to keep my cards close.

Sitting in the truck I checked my phone. Allie had returned my message with a smiley face and Justine's message asked if I was still around and if I wanted to have dinner. I called her right back and we decided on a restaurant and time. I had about an hour to kill and it only took fifteen minutes to get to the restaurant. On a hunch, I entered the address on Shelton's business card into the map app on my phone. It told me eighteen minutes.

The app took all the guesswork out of the drive. It calculated the fastest route and all I had to worry about was not crashing. This gave me some time to think. The drawing in my pocket was a surprise and I wasn't sure what to do with it. There was no doubt that Burkett knew his business and was correct; the question was, why had he given it to me—something I had not wanted to ask with a room full of Miami-Dade detectives sitting next door expecting a confession.

I needed to figure it out on my own. Sitting at a red light, I took the page out of my pocket and stared at it, wondering how finding the sections of debris that had been blasted would change anything. The light turned green and I started following the directions from my phone again. The way the computer voice gave me directions brought to mind working with my dad.

During summer breaks while I was in high school, I had started as a laborer for him then moved up to a carpenter. Then after a failed stint in college I had worked as a foreman until I joined the park service. It was all about the process and procedures he repeated over and over. "Measure twice and cut once" was all good advice, but it was the sequence you followed that separated the good carpenters from the bad. If you didn't brace the walls, then string and line the structure, the roof was not going to go on right. I assumed it was the same thinking when you were building a bridge.

An expert would be a big help and I pulled into the parking lot of a small strip center and made a quick U-turn. They might have had the knowledge, but I also remembered my dad cursing out the architects and engineers who'd had no idea how to actually build anything. Calculating the strength of a structure and actually building it were two different things entirely.

A gas station occupied the corner of the next block and I pulled in, parked, and tried to find

Willis's phone number. He might be young, but he had the background to answer my questions. I found his number and sent him a quick text asking if he wanted dinner. It turned out to be an offer he couldn't turn down.

After pulling back into traffic, I drove to the restaurant. Justine's car was already there when I arrived. I parked and went inside, hoping to have a few quiet minutes with her before Willis arrived. I found her at a corner booth and slid in beside her. After a warm kiss, she looked at me as if I was doing something wrong. We had moved on from the sitting side-by-side phase of our relationship a long time ago.

"Sorry to bring work to dinner, but I have a guest coming." I saw the look on her face when I said it and scolded myself for putting work first again. It had been my downfall before.

"Some *us* time would be nice, too," she said.

I was planning on staying at Adams Key tonight

as well to get an early start with Ray in the morning, but changed my mind. I was going to make this up to her. Willis was at the hostess stand and I waved him over.

"That's gonna be expensive," Justine said, watching him walk over to the table.

As he slid in across from us, I pulled the table a little closer to us to give him some room. After introducing him to Justine, we immersed ourselves in the menu. Justine and I had our standard order. I glanced across the table at Willis and saw the troubled look on his face. "I already saw you eat. We can share a bunch of stuff if you want," I said, thanking myself that we had decided on Chinese food. He smiled, knowing he was not going to go hungry, and we ordered.

After the first plates were cleared I pulled out the drawing and showed it to him. It stayed on the table as we tore into course number two, but as I watched him eat, I saw he was studying it.

“’You were to blow a bridge, those would be the spots.”

“Why?” I asked the question that was costing me dinner.

“Got cold joints there. The adjacent sections are the ones built in place.” He pointed to the abutments. “These here are wheeled in with heavy equipment and attached with tension rods.”

I had the procedure, but he wasn’t finished. Course number three interrupted the conversation. Justine and I had both exceeded our calorie limit for the week and started picking at our food. Willis continued on. When he was finished, we boxed up the remainder and I placed it in front of him. “Can’t have any starving students.”

“Appreciate that,” he said, moving the boxes to the side and setting the drawing in the center of the table. “I heard all that talk about the tension rods being over-tightened. You want to prove that it was otherwise, this would be the area to look.”

That was all well and good, but they were in a pile sixty feet underwater. "I'm going to help Ray set the mooring balls in the morning. I guess I can have a look then."

"You're going diving without me?" Justine folded her arms across her chest and made a face.

I recognized an opportunity when I saw it. "Of course not."

Chapter 19

Ray was pacing the dock when we came down the next morning. I checked my watch to see if we were on time; it was just six, our agreed on time. Ray must have abided by the same doctrine as my high school football coach: on time is ten minutes early. His boat was loaded with buoys, line, and tools, including a large gas-powered compressor. We had decided to take two boats, both for the added space and in case we ran late; then Justine could head back in the extra boat and get to work in time. With a grunt that might have been "good morning"—or not, he left the dock first and we followed.

I could feel Justine at my side and the worry about the case was far from my mind as we headed into the rising sun. Shades of yellow and red illuminated the small wind waves as they came toward us and a brilliant sky brought the dawn. The beauty was short-lived; by the time we reached the site, the sun was clear of the horizon and I could already feel its heat.

We stood off as Ray dropped anchor in the sand and paid out line, allowing the current to push the boat over the wreck site. The visibility looked good, but with the sun still low in the sky, I couldn't see the bottom. He signaled when the anchor was secure and I idled over. Justine dropped my fenders as I maneuvered around to his port side. The boats met and we quickly secured them to each other.

"Gear on up. Got a lot to do."

Ray was a man of few words, but I needed to know what he expected from me once we were under. After only a dozen or so dives, I was still a little nervous about working underwater and wanted a full briefing and a review of hand signals before we dove. "How's this going to work?" I asked.

He came over with his coffee mug and sat on his gunwale. Justine and I situated ourselves across from him on my boat.

"I'll carry the drill down, y'all take the anchors and line. Girlfriend here will keep everything from getting tangled." We had already decided that it would be easier to drill and use expansion bolts to attach the moorings to the bridge parts, rather than to haul out the large blocks of concrete often used to anchor the moorings.

My shoulders were tense as I dropped the buoyancy compensator over the steel cylinder and attached the regulator. Turning on the air, I checked the gauge, then scrolled through the screens on my dive computer, which confirmed that our bottom time at this depth could be as much as sixty minutes before decompression stops were required. From my previous experience and Ray's assurance, we wouldn't have to worry about time. Doing physical work underwater, our air would expire well before the hour was up.

Justine checked my gear and nodded. We were ready to go and I moved to the starboard gunwale, ready to drop into the water. She handed me the drill and I looked over at Ray before rolling over the side. He gave me a thumbs-up and splashed as his tandem tanks broke through the surface. He would be diving with twice the air that I had in a Nitrox mixture, which would allow him additional bottom time. When my air expired, I would surface and switch places with Justine while he remained below.

I gave him a few seconds' head start, gathered some extra hose, and rolled over the side. In addition to the weight of the drill and hose, Ray had me add weight to my BC to make it easier to work on the bottom. Instead of the eight pounds I usually carried when diving without a wetsuit, I had twelve. At thirty feet below the surface, the rubble came into view and I steered myself to a spot in the sand near Ray. With the additional weight, the bottom came up fast, and I inflated my BC to slow the descent.

He had warned me about stirring up silt if I tried to walk on the bottom and I added another blast of air to the BC. It took a few adjustments before I found the right amount of air to attain neutral buoyancy and I was now floating a few feet above the sand. As I approached him, Ray motioned for me to stop about ten feet away and started drilling the first hole. The air-powered hammer drill easily powered through the concrete and he inserted a large expansion bolt that had been clipped to his vest in the new hole. With a wrench he tightened the nut at the top and after it was secure, he motioned for the line, which he secured to the bolt.

With the first buoy set, we moved on to the next location about a hundred feet away. The work, especially my part, soon became routine and I started to notice my surroundings. Sea life had already been attracted to the beginnings of a slime coat that would eventually encourage the growth of coral and sponges. In a few years the only evidence that this had been a manmade structure would be its straight lines. Small fish swam in the open and through the gaps in the rubble, secure now, but soon enough the predators would find them.

I checked my watch and air gauge. After only thirty minutes I was down to 700 psi. We had decided that with the boat directly overhead, we would make our ascent at about 250. Ray was still working on the second hole. He was having a harder time with this one and I wondered what the difference was. Moving closer to him I ran a gloved hand over the concrete. This was a large section that had not failed, but rather had been broken with machinery to allow it to be loaded. I wanted to go back to the first hole and see what was different about that concrete, but Ray was ready to set the anchor. By the time the second mooring was secure, it was time for me to surface. I signaled to him and started my ascent.

With the extra weight I misjudged the expansion of the air in the BC and once I reached twenty feet, I started to shoot to the surface. I started to panic, recalling from my training that uncontrolled ascents were the leading cause of embolisms. Finally my left hand found the inflator hose. I held it over my head, and released some of the air. Under control now, I floated up to the surface and finned over to the dive ladder.

Justine helped me aboard and we quickly swapped gear. Taking two lines with her, she rolled over the side of the boat, gave me the okay sign, and submerged. As she descended I paid out the precut lines with the buoys attached to her. While I waited for her to reappear, I thought about what I had seen.

A picture began to form in my head of the bridge parts lying on the bottom. I thought if I had some time that I could possibly identify the sections that Burkett had marked. It wouldn't solve the crime, but any samples would be legally obtained and admissible as evidence.

I saw a flurry of bubbles breaking the surface and a minute later Ray and Justine surfaced together. So far we were on schedule and after an hour of diving, we had set four of the balls. We had figured on setting half of the eighteen balls today and half tomorrow. If you did the math based on the four we had set in another hour we would be almost done for the day, but that didn't account for the nitrogen in our bloodstreams. Even with the increased oxygen in the Nitrox mix, Ray would still need an hour or two on the surface before he could dive again. Three dives each day would get it done without putting us in jeopardy of decompression sickness.

After Ray and Justine were aboard, the gear was swapped to fresh tanks and the spent ones stowed, I opened the cooler we had brought and offered around sandwiches and water. Ray, true to form, finished his coffee and moved on to a small cooler full of beer he had brought.

While we drank, I asked Ray about retrieving a few samples.

"You know Martinez'll be up my butt if we don't get this done by tomorrow. Even though there ain't nothin to see here yet, they'll still be here in droves this weekend."

He was right. I had already seen several boats cruise by on my surface interval. "There's not a lot to do while you're drilling and setting the bolts. You're doing all the work."

"I can gladly hand off some of that to you. You guys are now official bolt setters."

I wasn't sure if the promotion helped or hurt the cause, but accepted it. Maybe with two of us doing the work, we could move faster. "Can we use any extra time to have a look around?"

"You get the quota done and you can play detective."

Also as SOP, Ray had set out a rod with a hunk of dead bait on a rig with a large weight after we had surfaced. Suddenly the reel buzzed and line started paying out. Ray took a long swig of his beer, crushed the can, and picked up the rod.

The tip bent over to the middle of the rod as Ray tightened the drag and started pumping the fish toward the boat. Several times he paused and allowed the fish to run, but he always seemed to know when to cut it short before the prey could entangle the line in the debris below. I hadn't seen any big fish down there, but if there was bait there would be predators.

"Kingfish, from the feel of him," Ray said, pumping hard. "Got him now. You want to come over here and get the leader?"

I hopped over the gunwale and waded through the lines and balls scattered on the deck of his boat. Leaning over the side I waited for the swivel to appear. I thought I saw it, but before I could reach down and grab the heavier leader, the fish must have seen the boat and made one last desperate run.

Ray was patient and allowed line to peel off the

rod, but as before, he sensed when it was near the bottom and tightened the drag. This time the fish came up easier and within a few minutes I could see the swivel again. Reaching over the side, I grabbed the line below it and wrapped it around my hand.

"No herky-jerky now. Just lift it," Ray cautioned.

With one motion, I straightened my body, lifting the fish from the water in the process and swung the large silver fish over the gunwale. Ray opened the lid of the cooler that also acted as a seat in front of the console and I slid the fish in.

"Best get back to work. Wouldn't be surprised if Martinez has a fleet of drones to go with his cameras," Ray said, eyeing a seagull that had been attracted by the fish.

Justine would have to leave for work soon and the surface interval had been plenty long to allow her to do back-to-back dives. I helped her with her gear and was ready with the lines when together they dropped into the water to fix the next two moorings.

When the lines went slack, I checked my watch. I expected they would be down longer this time. Justine had almost 800 psi of air left from the previous dive. It was Ray who had run out of air.

I figured forty-five minutes and settled in to wait. Pulling my phone out of the waterproof glove compartment in the helm, I checked my email and messages. Out this far there were only two bars of service and it took a while for the messages to come through. There was the usual good morning text from Allie, which I returned by sending her a picture of the mooring balls we had set bobbing in the small waves.

A minute later, the picture must have shown up on Martinez's screens and the phone rang with the Darth Vader ringtone Allie had downloaded for him. I answered, promising myself I was going to get a personal phone.

"Only four balls, Hunter? You guys fishing out there?"

Maybe Ray was right. "Should have half done by the end of the day. That was the schedule." I appealed to his bureaucratic sense rather than trying to explain about decompression times. I knew he wouldn't question Ray.

"Remember we're going to need you to work some overtime this weekend. Keep an eye on that new reef of ours."

It wasn't a question. I would have to figure out how to work it in with my promise to Allie and Justine to hunt lobster. I disconnected and watched the bubbles from the two divers working below as they popped on the surface. It looked like they had separated and I wondered if Justine was checking for evidence.

The mooring balls were like bait to flies. In the twenty minutes I waited for Ray and Justine to surface, I had to chase off three boaters looking to tie off. Finally, the volume of the bubbles increased as Justine dumped air from her BC on her ascent and when her head broke the surface I reached over the transom to help her aboard. There was something in her hand—a piece of concrete—which I set in the motor well while I grabbed the tank valve to help her aboard.

She spit out her regulator. “Got something.”

Chapter 20

With the chunk of concrete secure, I helped Justine aboard. She unclipped the BC and I took it and the tank from her. With the mask still around her neck she reached for the softball-sized chunk she had brought up.

"I'm taking this back with me to see if I can get anything off it," she said.

I looked over at it and saw the blasting cap intact in the bored hole. Not sure of the significance of the find right now, I started to gear up. Ray was still in the water and his impatience was apparent when the compressor on his boat fired up. He was already drilling the next hole and needed me to bring the lines down.

Justine was still looking at the piece while I geared up. I leaned in and kissed her before rolling overboard. The lines tightened and I wondered if she was still looking at her find and not feeding the slack overboard, but they soon loosened and I dropped to the bottom. Working my way over to Ray, I clipped the loops braided into their ends to my BC and started to help him. The hole was already drilled and he was in the process of fixing the bolt when he saw me. I could tell from his look that he had expected me sooner. I shrugged and had started to help when I heard an engine rev up overhead. Justine was heading back.

We were becoming more proficient at setting the buoys and I still had almost a thousand PSI left when the eighth ball was set. I motioned to Ray that I was going to ascend and get another setup. He nodded and started drilling the next hole. At this rate, even with the surface interval he would need after this dive, we would be done by mid-afternoon—plenty of time to get back to Miami and see what Justine had found.

I added air to my BC and started the ascent. The experience was paying off and I was soon back at the boat. After grabbing another line, I dropped back in the water. Glancing at my air gauge, I saw I still had 900 psi left and felt a sense of accomplishment that I was doing better with my air. Ray was ready for the line when I reached him and after affixing it to the bolt, we both surfaced.

With only three balls remaining aboard his boat, there was enough room for both of us and we sat at the console eating lunch. Ray finished off his beer and started working with his dive watch.

"Another twenty minutes and we can finish this off," he said.

I looked at my own watch and saw that we had only been up for forty-five minutes. The watch automatically calculated bottom times for different depths and after scrolling to sixty feet, I saw that I had fifty minutes. At the rate we were going that would be plenty of time to set three balls. Ray had been down a lot longer and I wondered how close to the edge he was cutting it, but with his experience and the Nitrox mix, I had to trust him.

A few minutes later we started to gear up; at twenty minutes, we dropped into the water. It was a little more complicated without someone on the surface managing the lines, but I had been careful to check the coils and they came cleanly into the water. We reached the bottom and started back to work, finishing the three balls in less than a half hour.

Back aboard we stowed the gear and hauled the airline and drill to the surface. Ray started the engine and I was about to head to the bow to help with the anchor when I saw him pick up his phone. He checked his messages and turned the power off.

"Might want to turn yours off, too."

What Martinez didn't know wouldn't hurt him, and I figured that he would be confused enough with Justine taking my boat back earlier. I shut mine off as well and went forward. As Ray idled toward the anchor, I took in the slack and motioned to him when we were directly over the hook. He slowed and I started to haul on the line. Using hand signals I showed Ray which way the line was running as he drove over it. When it was perpendicular I raised my hand in a fist and he stopped. Sitting directly above it, the anchor came aboard easily. He wasted no time and as soon as I was by his side, pushed the throttle down. The propellor dug in and slowly the bow started to come down and our speed increased as we came up on plane.

I had just started to work on the puzzle pieces in my head when we arrived back at Adams Key. Becky, Jamie, and of course Zero were standing by. Zero sniffed the air but seeing no sign of Justine or Allie collapsed in a grassy area shaded by a palm tree. He hadn't quite come to grips with Jamie and gave the toddler a wide berth.

I helped Ray unload and clean the boat while Becky took the fish to the cleaning table by the side of their house. Zero, seeing an opportunity for scraps, sauntered over to her and dropped by her feet, ignoring Jamie who had gone with her.

"You want to load up for tomorrow?" I asked.

"Nah, stuff happens around here and I'm guessing you want a ride back to headquarters."

"Appreciate it." Justine had taken the boat to Dodge Island, where she would get a ride or take an Uber to work. I was either going to leave it overnight and get Ray to take me over tomorrow, or see if he would give me a ride to my truck. Thinking about the piece of concrete Justine had found and what it could mean to the investigation, I was glad that he had offered.

"Becky has some shopping to do. Go on and get cleaned up. We'll leave in thirty minutes."

I thanked him again and went upstairs to my living quarters. A cold drink and quick shower reinvigorated me and I went back to the dock to wait. Zero was not present and I guessed not happy when

Ray, Becky, and Jamie boarded the boat. I sat on the cooler in front of the console to give them more room. It was a slower ride with the family aboard and I planned my escape as the boat cut through the light chop. Avoiding Martinez had become a priority after he had pulled the plug on the case.

With my boat at Dodge Island and my phone still powered down, Martinez had no idea where I was. Now I just had to stay clear of his arsenal of security cameras and get to my truck. I figured as soon as I left headquarters he would figure it out, but evading him now would get me on the road without a confrontation.

I remained on board for a few minutes after Ray and his family left. When I saw Ray's truck pull out of the lot, I made my move. It appeared I had gotten away cleanly and I kept my phone off until I was on the Turnpike, but when I turned it on there was a message waiting.

It was close to four. With an hour until the news

broadcasts, I decided this might be a good time to call him back.

"You need to stay within the lines," Martinez said.

I already knew what he meant. Justine taking the boat without permission had not been a good idea. "Half the buoys are set. We'll get the rest tomorrow with no problem."

"Of course you will. I'm assuming your girlfriend took the boat back to Dodge Island. That is against regulations."

He had allowed her to run the boat before, when we'd rescued Susan McLeash and a party of kayakers she was leading. I decided to use this. "She's run the boat before and this was official business." I explained about her finding the concrete chunk with the blasting cap intact. "This is looking like a murder and I don't want any bad press to come down on the park for dumping the debris so quickly." I made my point, leaving him an out in the process.

"At least your priorities are in order."

I breathed out. It had worked.

"Keep me posted." He disconnected.

I figured he'd be on his way out the door to watch the news at whatever bar his golf buddies frequented. At least for now Martinez was off my plate. With the clock closing in on five p.m.—when Justine would be alone at the lab—I switched to the left lane and accelerated. Traffic was at a standstill in the southbound lanes, and though the northbound lanes were moving near the speed limit, I knew there would be a stretch after I passed 836 where I would face the same. The east–west connector split Miami in half and I was moving toward it; pretty soon I would be in the middle of the northbound exodus from downtown Miami.

As I drove, I started to wonder what having the piece of concrete with the intact blasting cap meant. At least it was admissible evidence, but I couldn't figure out how it would help further my case. I already knew someone had timed the collapse to when Larry Shelton was below it.

There was one option where it might prove useful. Burkett was still in jail and Roslyn was sure to know it. If she was ever going to let her guard down, this might be the time. Usually investigators like to keep their evidence close so the suspects are not sure what they have and what they are guessing at. I thought trying the opposite with her might work. By revealing to her what we had found, I hoped I could elicit some kind of reaction from her.

I waited until I saw the brake lights ahead and slowed. With the wheel secured between my knees, I found her contact information and called her. I wasn't surprised when she didn't pick up. I had given her one of my cards, but wouldn't have expected her to enter it into her contacts. I rarely answered random numbers either. When the voicemail greeting ended, I left her a message that we had found some evidence that I wanted her opinion on, left my number, and disconnected.

My guess was confirmed when less than a minute later my phone rang. "Thanks for returning my call."

"No problem. You said you had some new evidence? I thought Burkett was in jail already."

She sounded wary, but I had started the ball rolling and wanted to see where it would end up. "Same kind of thing, but I'd really like an expert opinion," I said, hoping the flattery would get me a meeting.

"I'm near the forensics lab. Does that work for you?"

Aside from having her and Justine within striking distance of each other it was what I wanted. "Great. I'm on my way." I disconnected. Now I had to warn Justine that she would be having company, especially if Roslyn beat me there.

"Hey," she answered.

"Get to work on time?"

“Yup, all good. The day shift is on their way out the doors. Thought I might have a look at that concrete.”

“I’m about twenty minutes out. Okay if I come by?”

“Sure. Just text me when you get here and I’ll buzz you in.”

I drew a deep breath. “Hope you don’t mind, but I asked Roslyn to come by as well.”

The line went silent. I knew she was upset, but I needed to keep her in the dark . Roslyn was nothing if not shrewd. If this was my one chance, I had to make it work. There were only a handful of cars and I wasn’t sure what Roslyn drove. “I’m outside. Have you seen her yet?”

Chapter 21

Justine was excited about her find, but I could tell she was also anxious about Roslyn. I did my best to both reinforce the importance of her being there and minimize the engineer's impact. I had put myself in a bind. The chunk of concrete with the embedded blasting cap would not yield much in the way of physical evidence. The saltwater would have erased any fingerprints or DNA. What it did accomplish was to add to the growing theory that the bridge had been blown up intentionally. But even if it was circumstantial, it would be admissible and it was as close to a smoking gun as we had. What I was really hoping for was a reaction from Roslyn that might tell me something.

I planned to watch her carefully, knowing the stone-faced engineer would be hard to read. But with indisputable evidence that her crusade against Burkett for over-tightening the tension rods was not the cause of the failure, there would have to be some tell—either way. She would either know about it or it would be a complete surprise. The drama would be good enough to sell tickets and popcorn, if not to the public, then to slightly geeky special agents and forensic techs.

I thought about calling Grace and letting her know what I was up to, but then decided it would be better if she had deniability. Miami-Dade had an Internal Affairs department with teeth; all I had to worry about was Martinez. I was not ready to have Burkett released and he had been incarcerated on her authority. Knowledge of new evidence that might point away from him was a conflict of interest for her.

The audience would be Justine and me, and Justine had no idea what I was up to. We heard a buzz, and Justine went to the lab door. Roslyn stood there impatiently. She must have had a visitor's pass that allowed her access to the building but not the lab.

I remained where I was, moving my body to shield the chunk of concrete from her view.

"Agent Hunter," she said.

Justine looked annoyed and moved me out of her space. This might have gone better with the two of us if I had told her about my ploy, but Roslyn was anything but a fool. Her radar ran on high-power 24/7.

The silence dragged on for too long.

"You want to tell me why you called me over here?"

I almost pushed Justine out of the way to show Roslyn the concrete sample. Once it was in plain view, I stood by watching her. If you could call clinical interest a reaction, that's what the look on her face was. It was as if her features were frozen.

"And how does this fit into the bridge collapse?"

I explained about finding the blasting cap in Burkett's pocket, carefully leaving out the part that he was drunk. The guy was under heavy enough fire; he didn't need a strafing run. Then I told her how Justine had found the chunk of concrete that was sitting on the table.

"That's all well and good, but it still points to Burkett. Maybe I was wrong that over-tightening the bolts had caused the failure. Maybe it was still him, but he blew it up."

"You're sure about that?"

"You said you found the blasting cap in his pocket."

I didn't want to let on that I was convinced of his innocence and didn't tell her about his visit to the barge. What I wanted from her was the smallest doubt that Burkett was at fault. "No one else could have placed it?"

"There's people crawling all over that job: carpenters, laborers, concrete finishers, testers…"

She said it as if they were monkeys.

"And what about the man that was killed?"

"That was unfortunate."

I should have known not to expect any show of compassion from her for the dead man or his family. Plan A had failed and I found myself standing between the two women with no Plan B. Another long silence came over us.

"I can see that you're trying to do the right thing here, Agent Hunter," Roslyn said, putting her hand on my arm and smiling. "But if there is nothing else, I'll be on my way."

She left without a word to Justine, who stared after her. I could feel Justine's eyes boring through her on the way out the door, because when Roslyn left, she turned and leveled them on me.

"And you…if you're going to set someone up in front of me, you damned well better let me know first. You used me."

There was no whine in her voice. It was a cold

hard accusation and I knew better than to rebut it. “I’m sorry. I was trying to see her reaction.”

“The woman’s in this up to her emerald freakin’ green eyes. Maybe if you looked past them you’d see what is really going on here.” She turned back to her table. “I have work to do.”

The dismissal hurt, but I had earned it. I knew her well enough to know that there was no going back tonight. The best outcome for me was to let her work and talk to her in the morning. I said good night to her back and left the lab. My head was down when I walked out the front door and was surprised when I heard my name.

“Agent Hunter, you look like you could use a drink.” Roslyn started after me.

I did and I didn’t. Under different circumstances, and if Justine hadn’t been less than a hundred feet away, I might have said yes. I badly wanted to get into her head. I had a moment of indecision, questioning whether my relationship with

Justine was affecting my work and decided it was, but at the same time realized that she was more important to me than my job. "I'll pass, but thank you."

"Well, you have my number if you change your mind," she said and turned to walk away.

Even though I knew she knew that I was watching her, it was hard not to follow the swing of her hips. Thankfully, my phone vibrated in my pocket, forcing me to look away. Glancing at the screen, I saw it was a text from Allie. Her timing was too good, and I had the feeling that both of the women in my life were teaming up against me.

Defeated, I texted Allie that I was busy and wished her good night. I didn't want to expose her to my current state of mind. I left the crime lab, heading back to the headquarters building. Deep in thought, it was only when I was halfway to Homestead that I remembered that my boat was at Dodge Island where Justine had left it, and realized that she still had the keys. But I continued south, knowing that Mariposa had an extra set behind her desk. By morning, however, both she and Martinez would know I had taken them so I decided on the next best case—using Susan McLeash's boat to get home. Justine needed her space and it was better than driving all night to retrieve the keys and then heading back to Miami.

I reached headquarters and looked down as I passed the camera and unlocked the door. At Mariposa's desk, I found the extra keys and took both Susan's and mine then headed out, locking the door behind me. After boarding her boat, I started untying the extra lines that she used. When there were two remaining, I started the engine and checked the fuel gauge. It was standard procedure and good sense both for the stability of the gas and to be ready in case of emergency to keep the tank topped off. The needle hovered below the quarter-full mark and with the inaccuracy of fuel gauges in boats it could be less. I estimated there were a little less than twenty gallons. I would have to run slower to conserve fuel, but I figured I had plenty to make it out to Adams Key and back again. This was just another example of the common sense things not laid out in the manual that she chose to ignore.

It had taken some time to overcome my aversion to boating at night, but I tended to enjoy it now. The feeling of gliding over the ink black water with the low outline of the barrier islands and stars beyond reaching out to infinity could usually put any problem I was having on the back burner. Tonight was different, which only reinforced what Justine had come to mean to me.

I reached Adams Key feeling dirty, not from the day, but more from the way I had treated her. Using the current, I cut the motor well out from the dock and quietly set the fenders over the side while the boat drifted over. The last thing I wanted was to wake Zero.

At least I was able to accomplish that, or more

likely he had picked up a cosmic vibration that I was alone and now he was mad at me as well. I dragged my bad mood upstairs and drank a beer. Before going to bed I took one more look at my phone, hoping that Justine had called while I had been making the crossing. As expected there were no messages on the screen and went to bed.

I woke up surprised that I had slept, after tossing and turning for most of the night. A glance outside showed an ominous sky with grey and black streaks running through it. I reached over for my phone to check the time and saw it was almost seven. Jumping out of bed, I dressed and made two peanut butter and jelly sandwiches; one I ate on the way to the dock, the other was lunch.

I could hear the sound of Ray's engine before I reached the dock. It was too loud and I knew something was wrong. Looking up at the coconut palms planted in clusters around the clearing, I noticed the fronds whipping back and forth. When I reached the open walkway the wind hit me hard. The weather gods were apparently adding their opinion of how I had treated Justine. It was too early to call her, but I promised myself I would reach her before she went to work.

"Gonna be a little bumpy out there," Ray said from the deck of his boat. He looked over at Susan's center console. "What'cha got, ole Susan stashed up there? Her boat, ain't it?"

"This weather she won't miss it."

"Got that about right."

"I'm gonna grab my rain gear," I said, heading back to the house. When I returned he was ready to go. I boarded and pulled my ball cap down hard on my head. Ray looked over at me and I released the lines and pushed off from the dock.

He must have noticed my apprehension. "Once we get in the water it'll be all right," he said.

The ride to the new reef was as advertised and despite the rain slicker, I was drenched. Figuring he was going to be wet in a few minutes anyway, Ray stood stoically behind the wheel the whole time.

The mooring balls we had set yesterday became visible and he idled up to the site. "Grab the boathook. We might as well use one of those balls we set yesterday. Use that fifty foot of line I got out there. Extra scope'll make it a little easier on us up here."

I followed his directions and tied off to the buoy. After feeding the fifty feet of line out, I noticed the boat was rising and falling with the waves without the extra jerk that you felt when at anchor. I turned to Ray, who was almost ready to dive, and joined him in the stern where I slid into the waiting BC with the tank and regulator already set. Breathing in through the regulator, I gathered my mask and fins and prepared the lines. Ray had already lowered the hose for the drill over and started the compressor.

Despite the mooring ball and fifty foot of scope, the four-foot seas tossed me around the boat, causing me to fumble with my gear. Ray waited patiently, but finally disappeared over the side. I stuck the regulator in my mouth and followed.

The extra weight quickly dropped me below the swells and I started to relax. At twenty feet there was no indication of the sea state above and I tried to focus on the work ahead. Ray was already on the bottom, moving the drill and hose to the next location. I followed and waited while he bored the first hole.

We had talked about doing things differently today to save some time and to reduce the number of dives. Instead of drilling the hole, setting the bolt, and securing the line for each buoy, he had decided to do all ten in sequence.

The new procedure had me drilling every other hole and the needle was pegged into the red on my air gauge when we finished the last one. I tapped the gauge so Ray could see and started up hoping I had enough air left to reach the surface. Halfway there, I heard the unmistakable sound of an engine. It is virtually impossible to tell the direction of sound underwater, but you can hear proximity.

When it finally stopped, I had the feeling that we had company.

Chapter 22

The seas above us should have deterred most recreational fisherman or divers. Unless they already had a charter, even the commercial guys would have been thinking twice about going out today, making me wonder who would be in the boat now hovering above us. Until the reef had a chance to become established there were much better fishing and diving spots.

Ray must have suspected something was odd as well because he gave me the thumbs-up sign for us to surface. Leaving the weighted lines and drill on the bottom, we slowly started our ascent. When we were ten feet off the bottom I saw something coming toward us from the surface. My first thought was of that scene from too many dive movies when the bad guys start to throw meat and blood overboard to attract sharks.

It turned out I wasn't far off. Sinking quickly, the first package hit the concrete and exploded. It was followed by several others. Before I could figure out what was going on the concussion from the blast hit me and spun me upside down. I swatted at the inflator hose on my left side, intending to inflate my BC and rise above the fray, but it wasn't where it should have been. After a half dozen explosions the water was full of silt, which only added to my vertigo.

Remembering that I was almost out of air, I forced myself to relax and regulate my breathing. Just as I started to regain my wits my head hit something hard. A little woozy, I tried to figure out where I was. Visibility was near zero and I used my hands to survey the area around me. Feeling sand, I realized I was on the bottom. The initial blast had blown me away from the reef.

Knowing I didn't have enough air to wait until the silt settled, I pressed the inflator button and added enough buoyancy to allow me to float off the bottom. As I moved up through the water column I assessed my condition. My ears were buzzing from the blasts and I checked my limbs. Finding everything working, I started to fin toward the surface. Twenty feet from the bottom, the silt suddenly cleared and I checked my surroundings.

It was the same feeling as looking out the window of an airplane at the clouds below. The water was clear around and above me, but when I looked down there was a silt layer disguising the bottom. Now that I knew I was okay, I started scanning the water for Ray. The layer of silt still hung in the water and I couldn't see him anywhere around. I was about to descend until I took my next breath and felt a slight restriction. I didn't need to check my gauges to know I only had a few breaths of air left. This left me no choice but to surface.

At ten feet, I felt the surge from the seas above and I looked up, trying to find the boat. Yesterday at this depth the hull had been easy to spot, today with the waves passing overhead, I couldn't see it and started to get anxious. With each breath it was becoming harder to inhale and I felt the last drop of air enter my lungs as I pushed through the surface.

A wave immediately crashed over my head and I pressed the button to inflate the BC. Nothing happened and I gasped for another breath just as a large wave took me under the surface. It took two more waves until I remembered my training, and after taking a deep breath that was half sea water, I expelled it into the mouthpiece on the hose. The BC slowly inflated and several breaths later, I was bobbing on the surface.

Another moment of panic struck when I saw nothing in front of me except white-capped waves and the transom of a boat moving away. I squinted through my fogged-up mask, but couldn't read the name stenciled on the back. About to lose the only chance to see who had done this, I pulled off my mask and stared at the boat. It was a sportfisher, similar to Burkett's, but larger with a turquoise bottom. I could barely make out the lettering on the back: *Mud Man*.

Now that I had a name, I needed to find Ray and survive this. I had been in dangerous situations before and knew I had to get control of my emotions. With the BC acting as a flotation device and keeping my head above the waves, I was out of immediate danger, allowing me to assess the situation.

Finally, after several minutes, I could feel the adrenaline wane and my thought process slowly return. But I was angry. Wanting revenge is not healthy, and ultimately soul-sucking rather than satisfying, but in this case it fueled me and I rolled with it. The only way to get revenge on whoever was aboard the sportfisher was to find them. That meant I had to save myself and find Ray. I would deal with my feelings later.

Using my fins, I spun in a circle, finally spotting the three buoys we'd been getting ready to install. There was nothing else in sight. When I was in the troughs of the waves, it was impossible to see anything but water, but when I was lifted onto the crest, I could see a fair distance. The boat and the buoys we had secured yesterday were gone.

With nothing but ocean behind me, I flipped on my back and finned toward the cluster of buoys. They were floating freely with the current, but with their higher profile the wind was moving them faster than me. It took a few minutes of hard kicking to reach them and, out of breath, I grabbed for the line. Finally able to rest for a minute, I scanned the water and started calling out Ray's name.

I knew in this wind, whistles were often useless, but anything can give you hope. Reaching for the bright orange device, I alternated blowing into it and calling Ray's name. Without the air to descend or any sight of Ray on the surface, it was my only hope and

I continued.

Pausing to catch my breath, I thought I heard an engine approaching and redirected my energy in that direction. The noise was faint, but it sounded like it was upwind and I renewed my efforts, hoping my voice or the whistle would be carried toward it. A larger wave lifted me on its crest and I turned toward the sound. Before I crashed down into the trough, I saw a T-top. I was sure it was the forest green that the park service used. With everything I had, I blew the whistle. The next wave lifted me and I saw the bow turn toward me. It was my boat and Justine was at the wheel.

She came in on the downwind side and extended the boat hook toward me. I grasped for it, but the effect of the wind on the higher profile of the boat pushed it out of reach. Slowly, Justine circled back around and came in closer. This time I was able to grab the hook and she pulled me toward the dive ladder.

Grasping the stainless steel bar, I reached down for my fins and immediately felt my leg seize up. Exhaustion had been staved off by the adrenaline surging through me after the explosion. Now that I was within two steps of safety, cramps had started to set in.

"Just hang there for a minute. It'll pass," Justine called down.

I looked up at her. "I love you."

"I love you back, now get your butt out of the water." She reached down and grasped my tank valve.

I got a knee onto the ladder and reached behind me again. The change in position helped and I was able to remove one fin. I tossed it into the boat and with Justine pulling on the valve I was able to climb onto the small platform. Turning my back to the transom, I sat there breathing hard for a second before releasing the straps on my BC.

Justine pulled the tank and BC into the boat.

Free of the encumbrance, I was able to remove my other fin and climb aboard. “Have you seen Ray?” I asked as I collapsed on the deck.

“No, or his boat. I just saw those buoys floating and then heard the whistle.”

“He might still be under.” I tried to estimate how long it had been since the explosion and couldn’t decide whether time had stood still or moved faster. My watch solved the problem. It had been forty-five minutes into the dive when I started toward the surface. The stopwatch on my dive computer was still running. “Fifteen minutes. He could still be alive.” We had shared the workload this morning and I had no doubt he had more air than I did.

“Where’s the reef?”

“Should be the last waypoint on the screen.”

I moved to the bow while she drove toward the coordinates.

“Here,” she called out.

I waited until she turned into the seas. When she was about a hundred feet upwind I dropped the anchor. Rope followed chain and soon slack started to form. I tied off the line while Justine backed down to set the hook. There was no time to wait and see if it had set and I moved to the gear sitting on the deck. I reached for the tank and BC, but Justine shut me down.

"I'll go. Call for help."

She was right. Besides the nitrogen still in my blood, I had already started to cramp, and if Ray was down there and needed help, I would be unable to assist him. Justine still had her gear aboard from yesterday. I helped her gear up and turned on the tank valve. "You only have a thousand pounds left."

"Let's hope that's all I need."

It was the last air we had aboard.

I could still feel my muscles resisting as I helped Justine into the BC and watched as she rolled over the side. A second later there was no sign of her except a small stream of bubbles. After taking one last look, I stood, crossed to the console, and picked up the microphone.

With the VHF radio set to channel 16, I put out a call to the Coast Guard. There was no need to notify Martinez; he had a base station in his office. He would know as soon as they did. A response came immediately and I informed them of our location and situation. I could imagine Martinez sitting in his office, wringing his hands. Announcing this on the open airwaves was going to attract some negative press, but Ray's life was more important.

They responded that they were en route. Just as I put the microphone back in its holder, I heard my name through the speaker. It was Johnny Wells, the ICE agent that shared our dock space. I answered and we switched channels, something I probably should have done with the Coast Guard. The transmissions were still public, but interested parties would have to change channels as well.

He responded that his Interceptor was heading our way with an ETA of ten minutes. I had been aboard the thirty-nine-foot quad-powered boat before and seen dive tanks in a rack in the cabin. If he was only ten minutes away, they could aid in the search. I asked him to have divers ready and went back to the side of the boat.

The minutes passed slowly and with nothing to do but stare at the water and think I tried to remember anything I could about the *Mud Man*. It was a curious name and I had a feeling I had seen or heard of it before. Having spent over three-hundred days on the water that wasn't unusual, and I tried to recall where I knew it from. Just as the Interceptor pulled alongside, I found the memory. It was the name, really. People in the industry referred to concrete as mud, and I remembered the pictures on Brockmore's wall. It was his boat.

"How can we assist?" Johnny Wells called across as two of his men secured the boats together.

“Got a missing man. Justine is down trying to locate him.”

“Got it.” He had two men geared up and signaled for them to go. They rolled backward over the side and submerged.

I felt better knowing there were three divers looking for Ray and checked my watch. Justine had been down a half-hour. That was about the limit of her air.

As if on cue her head broke the surface, she signaled that she was okay, and finned to the ladder.

“He’s good. The other divers have him.” She spat out the regulator, gasped for air, and hung from the ladder while she caught her breath.

Knowing that she had found Ray and he was all right was a relief, and I let her rest for a minute before helping her aboard. The ICE agents came to the near gunwale.

“He was trapped under a piece of rubble. I think his leg is broken, but he still had air. With the other two divers, we were able to lift it off him. They should have him to the surface any second."

The ICE agents took positions port, starboard, and stern. One of them called out and they worked like the well-drilled team that they were to bring Ray aboard.

"We can get him in a lot faster." Johnny said as soon as the divers were aboard. Without waiting for an answer, he ordered his men to release the lines, spun the wheel and slammed down on the throttle. I had no idea how badly Ray was injured, but he was in a damned fast boat and in good hands.

The wake from the quads hanging from the transom of the Interceptor threw me against Justine and we stood together staring at the boat until it was lost in the waves.

Chapter 23

"I meant it," I said as we watched the horizon swallow the Interceptor.

"Meant what?" Justine asked.

I knew she was playing with me and I deserved it. It was time to step up. "That I love you." It was easier said the second time.

"And I meant it, too," she said.

The doghouse was too big to get out of with words alone, however. I put my arms around her and swung her into a deep embrace. Finding her lips, I kissed her long and hard. It quickly turned into a contest of who would release first. The moment had been building for a while. Unfortunately it had taken a life-or-death situation to get it out.

"You saved our lives."

"Ray doesn't deserve to die."

Saying it like she did meant that *I* might. I knew she was kidding in her way, but I got the message. Our fight from last night lay unresolved and I knew better than to bring it up now. Instead I turned my attention to the present.

"Ray should be okay. I should call Becky when I find out where they are going to take him."

"Yeah, probably ought to let your boss know, too. He was working. It should all be covered by workers' comp."

I decided to put that call off, but the decision apparently wasn't mine to make. My phone rang, something I would never have heard if we'd already been underway. Our delay had cost me.

"What the hell, Hunter?" Martinez started. "Susan's boat is at Adams Key and Ray's is drifting in the bay."

I had forgotten about Ray's boat. "Can you give me the coordinates? I'll go after it."

"And you will bring it back to headquarters and

we will have a conversation."

We would. I was feeling empowered after surviving the blast and telling Justine that I loved her. Between the euphoria of being alive and her response, I was ready to face the elephant in the room. It was time to deal with Martinez.

With the phone on speaker and with the engine idling, I kept the bow into the wind to allow Justine to enter the coordinates as Martinez read them off. When she had finished, she hit the GOTO button and the plotter calculated our course and distance.

Ray's boat was several miles off, floating with the waves toward Black Point Park. After checking that everything was secure, I swung the bow around and headed toward the coordinates. The boat would continue moving as we pursued it, but its course would remain the same. Once the compass needle matched the direction indicated by the GPS, I pushed down the throttle.

With an outgoing tide and the wind out of the

east, the waves were stacked behind us making it difficult to find a comfortable speed. Finally, I found that going with the flow instead of fighting it was the best option and tuned the rpms to the speed of the waves. Except for the stern fishtailing off some of the breaking crests, it was a more comfortable ride, but slow.

Justine spotted the boat first and we were soon floating fifty feet from it.

"Do you want to drive it, or should we tow it?" I asked her. A tow would be messy and slow going in these seas, but it was her call.

"I'll drive her in."

Although we'd be separated, that was the simplest way. I set my boat in gear and allowed the drifting boat some leeway. After it had passed us, I gave the engine some juice and ran up next to it. Justine hopped nimbly over the gunwale, landing squarely on the deck. I didn't wait for her okay, but moved off immediately, before the boats could damage each other.

Justine took the lead and I followed her to headquarters. The run in gave me some time to think about what had happened earlier. First, I needed to find out Ray's status. I glanced at my watch. It had been forty-five minutes since Johnny Wells had taken off toward Miami. The park service bay boats were generally perfect for these waters—except when the wind kicked up the seas. The ICE Interceptor was built for heavy seas and would easily have docked by now.

It was too loud to call while underway. With the combination of the wind blowing at fifteen knots and the engine noise being blown back toward me there was no way to make a call until we stopped. I wanted to call Johnny before I talked to Martinez; unable to signal Justine, I accelerated to pass her.

Justine, being Justine, took this as a challenge and started to match my speed and then pulled slightly ahead. I had to push the boat hard to catch her and when she finally glanced over I could see the competitive smile on her face. It disappeared when I signaled her to slow down.

We entered the channel that the headquarters building shared with Bayfront Park and I continued past the turn to our marina. Passing the deserted boat ramp for the park, I idled into the small turning basin for the public marina just beyond it. It was calm enough to talk here and we drifted together in the light current.

"I want to talk to Johnny and find out about Ray before seeing Martinez."

"Probably a good idea. I have to call my boss, too. Looks like I'm going to be late."

I felt bad about keeping her, but figured she could spin her tardiness as being related to the case. We each made our calls. The news about Ray looked promising. He had been taken to Jackson Memorial and Johnny was standing by with him. I thanked Johnny and dialed the medical examiner's office, which was around the corner. Sid had been a great advocate when Justine had been shot on another case. I hoped he would have time to run across the street and do the same for Ray.

Justine was still talking and I turned to her with a questioning look to see if everything was okay. She nodded and finished her call.

"All good. Actually, he had an idea that we should get a warrant to search the *Mud Man*. If you can get that going, I'm cleared to process it. We might find explosive paraphernalia or residue and I bet if we do that it'll match the blasting cap."

"Great idea." I turned away and backtracked to the park service marina, passing the empty slip where the ICE Interceptor lived. I silently thanked the crew for being out in this weather. Before reaching my slip, I passed Pete Robinson's FWC boat rocking in its slip, a testament to his laziness. I backed into my slip and tied off the boat. Justine pulled into the empty slip next to mine and I helped her tie off Ray's boat.

“I have to talk to Martinez,” I said.

“I’m going with you. I witnessed the whole deal.”

I had this feeling, as if it was my mother insisting on going to the principal’s office, but Justine was probably right. I had to put our personal relationship aside and act professional.

We entered the building and caught a quick wave from Mariposa, who mouthed something to Justine that I couldn’t catch. Heading upstairs I steeled myself for the confrontation. Martinez had gotten his reef and inside of twenty-four hours it had become a crime scene—that wouldn’t make him happy.

The door to his office was open and he waved us in, motioning to the two seats. He was on the phone, one of his usual ploys to set me on edge. While we waited, I tried not to look at Justine and act natural. She made it easy by checking her phone. I couldn’t help but notice that Martinez noticed her and I smiled inside. She might have been checking her Facebook feed for all I cared, but she'd turned his rudeness against him.

He hung up. "Tell me what the hell happened out there."

I recounted every detail. Before he could say anything about taking Susan's boat, I told him that Becky was on her way in with it. When I finished the room went silent and I could see the wheels turning in his head about how to play this to his advantage. I didn't care much about that now. Ray and I had almost been killed this morning, and I had a lead on who had done it.

"I want to get a warrant to search the *Mud Man*."

He looked thoughtful again. "You think whoever was aboard is responsible for the bridge collapse as well?"

I knew if he thought I was going to close the case he would do as I asked. "I need a motive, but if we can get a forensics match to the explosives, we can probably make an arrest."

He sat back and looked at his watch. I knew he was trying to figure out if he could get the warrant fast enough that the arrest would make the six o'clock news. "I know a judge. Head up there and I'll have it ready."

That was easier than I had anticipated, but did not satisfy my need to confront him. For now, I made peace with myself, but knew at the same time that I had unfinished business.

My thoughts turned to the *Mud Man.* Except for the fact that I didn't know where the boat was, I had gotten what I wanted. There were ways to find a boat that large and expensive, though. I started to rise when he cleared his throat.

"Take Susan," he said, dismissing us.

I felt like I was in a pickle between third and home, but there was nothing to do about it now. Susan was always a wild card, but I was so close to solving this. I had what I wanted. Justine and I got up to leave as he turned back to his monitors.

"What are we going to do with Susan?" Justine asked on our way downstairs.

"She might be able to run interference with Brockmore while we search the boat."

"That didn't work out too well last time."

Justine was referring to another case, one during which Susan had tried to seduce a suspect in order to get leverage. "This guy deserves her."

Rain clouds were forming on the horizon to the north as we left the building. That got me thinking that finding evidence on the *Mud Man* might not be as easy as I hoped if the boat had been hosed down by its crew. Even if it hadn't been, the rain would do their work for them.

"We need to find the boat. Can you call Johnny Wells and see what he can do?" I asked as we pulled out of the park service lot.

"Roger that."

Between the Interceptor's state-of-the-art radar

and its access to vessel-tracking websites, if the boat was still at sea, I was sure Johnny could locate it.

"No problem," Justine reported. "He'll call back when he finds it. Says Ray is okay too."

"Mind if we run by the hospital and see him?"

"I'd like that."

My phone chimed the Darth Vader ringtone I had assigned to Martinez. Justine looked over at me and I nodded. She entered my password.

"He has the search warrant."

I was surprised by his efficiency. Now all we needed was a location. Playing the odds, I expected we would find the boat in Miami. Just when we hit the Shula Expressway the ominous skies turned into a rainstorm, slowing traffic. Thunder struck, followed by several flashes of lightning nearby. It passed by the time we reached 836, where I turned east, but the sky told me that wasn't the end of things.

With the rough seas and now the thunderstorms rolling in, I doubted the *Mud Man* would be out. If it were docked, it would likely be in one of the high-dollar marinas just past the hospital, in the direction we were heading anyway. We reached the exit with still no word from Johnny.

With my credentials leading the way we were soon in Ray's room. His leg was in a cast, elevated by some kind of apparatus. Becky sat by his side holding his hand and trying to entertain Jamie at the same time. His other hand was on the morphine drip.

"How goes it?" I asked, never knowing how to start a conversation in a hospital room.

"Been better." He turned to Justine. "I wanna thank you for saving us."

"*De nada*," she said. Leaning over the bed she kissed his forehead. "How long are they going to hold you?"

"Got a specialist coming to have a look, but I'm breaking out of here tonight—one way or another."

"The hell you are." Sid entered the room.

"You the specialist?" Becky asked.

"No, the coroner," Sid said.

I'd never seen Becky blush before. She looked flustered, especially as the rest of us were laughing. "He's a friend. I asked him to come by and make sure Ray gets the best treatment."

"And a good thing you did." Sid started pecking at the computer in the corner until he gave up. "Access codes. Paper charts were so much more accessible." He got up and went to the door. "I'm going to find the doctor."

Stooped over and head down, he charged out of the room to fulfill his mission. Just as the door closed, my phone rang. The caller ID said it was Johnny Wells.

Chapter 24

I looked down at the screen, turned to Justine, and mouthed *Johnny.*

With the phone still ringing we said quick good-byes. Becky gave us a heartfelt "thank you" and embraced us both. Ray, who was immersed in his escape plans and the morphine drip, merely nodded. Jamie just stared at the computer monitor. He had just started playing games on Becky's phone and the continuous lines running across the screen had him hypnotized. With Sid running the show now, Ray would be in good hands. No one would want to mess with the old man.

I pressed *Accept* as soon as I was through the door. "Hey."

"Got something for you. Right now the vessel is at the Miami Beach Marina. Not sure if they have a slip there or are fueling up. I'll have eyes on in a few minutes."

"Thanks. We're over at Jackson Memorial. Should be there about the same time with a warrant."

"Fun times," Johnny said and disconnected.

I was glad he was involved, rather than having to rely on Miami-Dade for backup. Justine was by my side and I told her the location.

"Scene of too many crimes," she said.

She was right about that. The marina had been central in several of my other investigations. It was located on South Beach with easy access to downtown, the Intracoastal Waterway, and the Atlantic through nearby Government Cut. If you had the money, that was *the* location. "Ready?"

"Right behind you, Kimo sabe."

We left the hospital and took off toward the marina. Red lights immediately stopped our progress when we got on 836. I guessed there was a ball game in town and settled in for the wait.

“Use your lights,” Justine said.

The small park service truck had a mini light bar. Compared to the trend of nightclub lighting on emergency vehicles it seemed almost like a toy. Deciding there was no harm besides being embarrassed when no one obeyed, I hit the switch. The lights started flashing, but no one moved, and I wished I had a siren to go with it. But between the lights making me look at least semi-official and Justine gesturing out the open window, I was able to reach the shoulder. I guessed Martinez was going to get a few window repair bills when gravel spun from my tires as I accelerated.

I could see the irritated looks on the drivers of the other cars as I passed them. Many had their heads down, probably searching Amazon for a set of make-believe police lights for themselves while they waited. The shoulder abruptly ended when I reached the causeway and I wove back into the flow of traffic. We were in the clear now, past the stadium exit, and cruised over the bridge at the speed limit. After passing several cruise ships docked across the channel at the pier on Dodge Island, the view opened up. We went by a string of smaller islands with large houses on the left. South Beach and the marina were ahead.

I turned right on Alton Road and then right again into the marina parking lot. There was no need to hide our presence and I pulled up in a no parking area in front of several buildings. We left the truck there and ran around the corner to the marina, where I scanned the area for the ICE Interceptor or the *Mud Man.*

It was a big boat, probably close to sixty feet, that in most other marinas would have stood out, but here it was average size. Searching through the maze of masts and flybridges it was almost impossible to see past the first few boats. My phone vibrated in my pocket and I reached for it as we made our way toward the first of several finger piers.

"They're on the back side of the northernmost dock. Looks like there's a sign for Pier 1. Got their engine running like they're getting ready to head out."

For a boat that size, "heading out" might mean for the Bahamas. "Can we meet you at the fuel dock and come around by water?" I asked.

"Roger that. Hurry; they're starting to throw lines."

I already knew that each finger pier had a locked gate. We would have to present the warrant to the dockmaster to gain access, but I knew most dockmasters were well taken care of by the boat owners, who expected them to provide privacy and security. If we ran into anyone other than Kyle or his sister, who I already knew, it would take too long. They would automatically delay us and try to reach the owner before letting us in. Going around by water, we'd also have the advantage of being able to blockade the *Mud Man.*

We ran to the fuel pumps, where Johnny was nosing the Interceptor's bow toward the dock. He stopped six inches short and I followed Justine aboard. Before I had reached the helm, he had already reversed and spun the wheel. Ignoring the idle speed signs, he accelerated toward the pier and turned on his light bar.

Not wanting interference or questions from adjacent boats, I would have preferred a quieter entrance, but when we rounded the corner, the *Mud Man* was just about to depart. Johnny called over the hailer for them to stand down, and slid the Interceptor broadside in front of the bow of the larger boat.

"We have a warrant. Secure your vessel and move all hands aboard to the dock," Johnny called over the hailer.

We had the attention of everyone in the marina as well as the passing boaters who had all stopped to watch the show. I got serious boat envy when Johnny used his bow thruster to hold the Interceptor in place while the *Mud Man*'s crew complied with his orders. A few minutes later, I could see three people disembark and line up on the dock. I relaxed my grip on the grab rail and moved to the port side where Johnny, seeing his orders were obeyed, slid the Interceptor toward the end of the pier.

Justine was just about to hop onto the dock when I saw movement down on the pier. Between the docked boats, I could see someone running for the gate. It looked like Brockmore. The gate slammed closed behind him and I took off at a run.

Justine was right behind me when I hit the paddle handle on the gate. The excitement had drawn a crowd, which worked to Brockmore's advantage, and he was quickly lost in the swarm.

"Let's split up," I said to Justine and headed south. She turned and went north. A few minutes later, both breathing hard, we met back at the gate. He had eluded us. I glanced down the pier and saw

Johnny had tied off the Interceptor and his men were standing guard over the crew. His boat was in our control, but Brockmore had likely reached his vehicle by now. We needed help and if he was on land, the only source I had was Miami-Dade.

"I have to call Grace," I said to Justine. "Can you show the warrant to the dockmaster and get him to open the gate?"

Grace answered my call and I gave her a brief rundown on what had happened. Her new partner must have been whispering bad things in her ear about me. I heard the tone of her voice change when I told her I only had a name—she had guessed I was using her even though she usually got credit for the arrests. But Grace was a pro and it only took her a minute to come back with Brockmore's vehicle registration and home address.

"I'm in the middle of something. It's going to take me a while to get there."

There was another way, though, and I thanked

her for the information then dialed Susan McLeash.

"Want to get in on the party?" I asked.

From the background noise it sounded like she already was.

"Give me a minute," she said.

The noise slowly faded until I guessed she was outside.

"Can you sit on a suspect?"

"Really? You want me to babysit?" she asked.

"Guy's got a sixty-foot boat and owns a concrete company," I inserted the high points from his resumé, thinking that should get her attention. "Name's Albert Brockmore." I gave her the address and told her what I wanted.

Justine was coming toward me with a dockmaster I didn't recognize and I disconnected before she could hear who I was talking to. He unlocked the gate and went back to the office, probably figuring that being seen with us would hurt his income stream. Justine and I walked to the end of the pier where the boat was docked. The two crewmen, a man and woman, were still off to the side.

"You want them in custody?" Johnny asked, handing me a piece of paper with their names and contact information.

I thought for a minute, studying the pair. They had the sun-worn, washed-out look of boaters. "Thanks, but I'll take it from here. Appreciate the help."

He nodded and went back to the Interceptor. Unlike Miami-Dade, there was no ego, drama, or the inevitable pissing contest. The ICE team was probably glad to help, but also happy to get out of here without any paperwork required. When I turned back to the crew, still standing on the dock, they looked relieved the ICE agents were gone as well.

"We've got a warrant to search the boat," I said, holding out the envelope containing the paperwork. Neither one moved and Justine climbed aboard.

There wasn't much for me to do onboard. She would call me if I were needed so I started asking the crew questions.

It turned out that the boat was normally docked up the Miami River. Not a long run from here, but surely in a less expensive marina. They had fueled up and were heading there when Johnny Wells stopped them. It didn't appear that Brockmore was trying to flee the country—at least not yet.

We spoke for a few minutes and they claimed ignorance of this morning's activities, saying that Brockmore had taken the boat out by himself, something he often did. He had asked the man who often captained the boat to meet him here; also, from what the male crewmember said, this was not unusual as the boat was a monster to dock alone. The woman turned out to be the man's girlfriend and had just gone along for the ride.

Double-checking their IDs against the paper Johnny had given me, I wrote down the marina and slip number where the boat normally docked and released them with the promise to call me if Brockmore contacted them. I checked in with Justine, who grunted back, a sure sign to stay away. Unlike the TV shows where detectives and techs would swarm a scene, she preferred to work alone. She was meticulous and would set up a search grid so that she could cover every inch of the area without contaminating it. When I walked away, she was about halfway through the cockpit.

I was walking away because I had an idea. Every marina had a neighborhood gossip and I just happened to know the resident one here—and where to find him. Gordy, owner of *Bottom's Up Boat Cleaning*, was at the bar in his usual seat. I didn't like the man or how he made his living by exploiting women. He hired them to clean boats in their bikinis, often offering more than the detailing package.

We had crossed paths before and I could tell by the look on his face that he felt the same way about me. I had not been able to tie him directly to any crimes, but he was always too close. If something had gone on here, I bet he knew about it. Trapped at the bar between two older women he was flirting with, I could see him squirm.

Standing back, I allowed him to extricate himself. I wanted information; embarrassing him, despite the reward, would get me nothing. We met at our assigned palm tree.

"Hello, Gordy," I started.

"Agent." He looked over at the bar like I should buy him a drink.

"Let's see if you can help first," I started. "*Mud Man*. Know the boat or the owner?"

When he smiled I saw the same ultra bright white teeth that Brockmore had. They both shared the same spray-on tan as well. There was no doubt they knew each other.

"Guy's a piece of work. What do you want to know? This one's on me."

I stayed quiet and let him continue.

"Keeps his boat at a low-rent place up the river and brings it around here for show. Too cheap for my services." He glanced over at the bar.

I guessed his offer of free information would require some lubrication. "The usual?" I asked. He nodded and I left him to order his drink. When I returned he took it and drank half through the small straw.

"I was saying. Word on the water is that things are not going so well for him. Concrete business, right?" He finished the drink in another sip.

I nodded and ignored his glance toward the bar. He would have to give me better information for a refill. He must have sensed the terms and continued.

"I saw him all liquored up at the bar a few weeks ago. Going on about this bridge and getting shut out of the concrete. It was a Saturday, I think. Started bragging about being called in to deliver some concrete and how they wouldn't forget him."

I remembered the *Open Saturday* banner on his building. The crews must have been working the weekend. That was all Gordy had, and I delivered his drink in return for the information.

On the way back to the boat, I stopped at the dockmaster's office to get him to open the lock for me and asked a few questions on the walk over. He confirmed that Brockmore often docked here to drink.

Justine was just finishing up in the cockpit and starting on the cabin when I returned. I called out to let her know I was back and sat on the white fiberglass dock box near the power pedestal. It was time to have another conversation with Burkett.

Chapter 25

As I'd feared, between the rain and crew, the decks had been washed clean of any evidence. I was starting to think this was a dead end. With the new evidence I had a feeling Burkett could provide some answers.

Justine emerged through the smoked glass door. With a smile on her face, she stood in the cockpit holding a roll of wire attached to a small cylinder. From where I sat I could see it was different from the blasting cap. This was fatter, with a round loop at the end opposite from the wire. It was a fuse igniter. Once pulled the ring would send a charge through the wire to the detonator. The length of wire determined the delay. From the coil attached to the ignitor, I guessed that these were set for about a minute—the perfect amount of time to drop a charge in the water and have it reach the bottom. With gloved hands, she slipped it into an evidence bag. "That's about all I can find, but it could be enough if there are prints or we can figure out where it was bought."

Due to the ability to buy anything over the Internet, the days of tracking down an item's retailers were pretty much over, but a fingerprint could be enough to get at least an indictment, if not a conviction.

Even if she had found the smoking gun, I still needed some backstory from Burkett. "How about I drop you at the lab and head over to county? I want to have a conversation with Burkett."

"Right on."

Justine looked excited about her find. My expectations were lower. We rode back to the lab and I pulled into the lot. We were both immersed in our own worlds, but I pulled her over before she could open the door and kissed her. She got out with a smile, and with the evidence bag in hand walked toward the entrance. Not wanting her to be accosted by the half-dozen reporters still camped out in front of the building would be my stated reason for delaying; the sway of her hips was the compelling one. I watched until she was inside.

I knew better than to go into the county lockup cold, and called Grace. She said she was tied up, but would make a call to the desk sergeant. I filled her in on what we had found and told her I thought it was time to release Burkett. There was a long pause on the line and I heard JT's voice in the background.

"Go on. I'll set it up," she said, and disconnected.

I felt bad that I had put her in a spot with her new partner, but some things were out of my control.

Burkett was being fast-tracked and had been moved to the pre-trial detention center. After reaching the building I parked and sat in the truck with the AC running, gathering my thoughts. Once I had a plan, I locked the truck and headed for the entrance. Grace had followed through, and after giving my name and showing my credentials to the desk sergeant, I was buzzed in and given directions to an interview room.

As an officer led me down the hallway, I looked at each room we passed, wondering when political correctness had trickled down to the corrections system. I could have sworn these were the same rooms that used to be called "interrogation" rooms. My escort stopped, keyed in a code, and opened one of the doors. When I entered, I saw Burkett sitting alone at the table.

"Might have some good news for you," I started, and sat opposite him. He didn't look up, and I studied the contractor. He was worse for the wear. The two days here had taken a toll on him, though I wasn't sure if having to dry out didn't have something to do with it.

"What would that be? They're going to arraign

me tomorrow morning and my public defender's an idiot."

I thought about telling him about Daniel J. Viscount, my five-figure-a-shot attorney. I had seen how deep his tentacles had reached into the system and what he could get done. Instead of the referral, I hoped that I could get Burkett released before any hearing occurred.

"What can you tell me about the concrete suppliers?" I asked.

His body language changed. "What do you want to know? You call them up and they deliver concrete."

"I'm here to help you. We've got some new information that is being processed as we speak that could vindicate you."

He looked up. "Really? I thought that bitch had a noose around my neck."

"She might, but she hasn't pulled the rope yet. Now, tell me about the suppliers, starting with the bidding process." I pulled out my pad and pen to show him I meant business.

"You really think this is going to help?" he asked. The defeated look was back.

I could have just asked about Brockmore, but I wanted the whole story. "Yes, I do." My phone vibrated and I held up a hand for him to hold on. It was a text from Justine saying that she had found something. I figured there was no harm in Burkett hearing it from her firsthand and called her back. Once the phone started ringing, I pressed the speaker button and set it face up on the table between us.

"Hey, we're on speaker with Burkett. I thought it might help if he heard it from you."

"There was a partial print on the detonator. I pulled what I could off and ran it through AFIS. It appears that Brockmore was in the military. His print is on the case."

Burkett was fully engaged now. "Albert Brockmore?"

"Yes, I went a little deeper and found out he was in demolitions. This stuff is his wheelhouse. Need me to go further?"

I recalled some of the pictures on his walls had been military. "I think we have enough for now. I'll get back to you when we're finished up here." I reached for the phone, but Burkett held up his hand.

"Thank you for doing this," Burkett said.

I could almost see the tear fall from Justine's eye. Yes, she was a geek, but also deeply cared about using her skills to get justice, rather than just solving riddles like many of the other techs. I looked across the table and Burkett nodded.

"Okay, I'll call you in a bit." I pulled the phone back and disconnected. "Got a story you want to tell me now?"

While he composed himself, I wondered if Susan had found Brockmore. The logical thing to do would be to bring him in for the attempted murder of two park service employees—Ray and me. He could claim that he hadn't known we were down there and get the charge downgraded to defacement of a public property, which was probably just a misdemeanor. But I decided to wait and get enough evidence to take him in for the murders associated with the bridge collapse.

Burkett started to talk and I wished I'd had a full-sized legal pad instead of the small pocket-sized one in front of me. He prefaced the actual construction process of the bridge by explaining the bidding process.

"The best guy doesn't always get the job, no matter how complicated it is. As long as a company can bond and produce the lowest bid, it is a rare case when they're not selected. You've got to bond. That's the whole deal. Bid bonds, performance bonds, payment bonds, and guarantees. It's harder to qualify and get bonded than it is to build the damned projects."

"How does that affect material suppliers?" I

asked.

"They usually don't have to bond specifically for the project, but they have to accept the terms of the contract and working for municipalities generally means a minimum of sixty and more likely ninety days before they get paid. And, that's the billing cycle, not when they did the work. It could be every bit of four months sometimes." He breathed deeply.

"Brockmore's bid was in line, but he wanted to get paid in thirty days. That would have forced me to use my line of credit. Why would I go with him when another supplier is okay with getting paid when I do?"

It was a rhetorical question, but I had an answer. "Because he'd deliver on Saturday."

"That might have been a mistake, but I was desperate. The job had liquidated damages and the school was not cooperating on extensions."

"Liquidated damages?"

"You accept the project with a given amount of

days to complete it. After that, every day the project comes in late there's a fee. Some fees run into the thousands a day."

I understood how that could influence his decision-making process. "So, you were running late and the supplier you had contracted with wouldn't or couldn't deliver on a Saturday, so you called Brockmore."

"It was a cost / benefit decision. Paying him right away, even if I had to go to my credit line and pay the interest was less expensive than two days of damages for being late."

"I guess stuff like this happens all the time?"

"Pretty commonplace. But I think Brockmore got the mix wrong. His yard wouldn't carry the fly ash specified. He'd have to bring it in. My feeling is that he substituted an inferior product. We questioned it at the site, but the engineer did his slump test, which fell within the project parameters. That just shows the consistency and not how good the mix is. The other tests take twenty-eight days to allow the concrete to cure."

"Why didn't you stop the pour?"

He raised his hands. "I'm just a poor contractor—the low man on the totem pole. If the engineer says go, we go."

"You know the name of the engineer who did the testing that day?"

"Larry Shelton. He was one of the better ones." His eyes opened wide. "Do you think he got killed for this?"

It was too early to confirm, so I waffled. "We're looking into it."

I rose and said I would do what I could to get him out. Leaving the room, my feeling was that if Burkett was guilty of anything it was not yelling "time-out" loud enough. He hadn't committed a crime, whereas Brockmore, at the least, had tried to blow Ray and me up. I left the building thinking that if Justine didn't have the smoking gun, I thought I might. Larry Shelton had been killed to hide the bad concrete. Now, I needed the test cylinders to prove it.

Checking my watch as I got into the truck, I saw it was close to five, and on a Friday, that meant I had to get to the testing facility before they closed or I would have to wait until Monday. After entering the address into the maps app on my phone, its calculation showed I didn't have a chance. I had one option open to me and paused before I found Roslyn Maya's number in my call log.

"Receptive" was not a word that I would have used to describe her, but she proved me wrong. It occurred to me as I sat in Friday rush-hour traffic that if her tester had been killed for possibly being a whistleblower, her firm would come out of this looking good no matter who had actually killed him. In her view it was still Burkett's fault for using Brockmore's concrete in place of the regular supplier's.

I finally reached the testing facility a half-hour after they officially closed, but Roslyn was waiting in her car by the entrance. She got out and led me to the door, which she opened by entering a code into a keypad. I followed her in. The place reminded me of Brockmore's offices: totally utilitarian. She led me through a door off the small waiting room, where the magazines looked at least ten years old, and into a large warehouse.

Tens of thousands of dollars' worth of equipment was lined up against one wall, and racks full of six-inch diameter by foot-long cylinders covered the opposite wall. At the end of the space there were two roll-up garage doors. Roslyn went to a light switch and suddenly the dim room came to life.

"This is all our testing equipment," she said, starting the tour.

"Can we locate the cylinders for the bridge, specifically from the Saturday when Brockmore supplied the concrete?"

"No foreplay for you," she said, leading me across the concrete floor to the steel racks.

They were sorted by date and it didn't take long to find what we were looking for, or rather the location of what we were looking for, because the dates jumped…from Friday to Monday.

Chapter 26

Roslyn's stone facade crumbled and I could see she was shocked to see the samples were missing. In that moment, she seemed almost human. Moving through the rows of stainless steel cylinders she became more and more frantic as she searched. If my theory was correct she wouldn't find them. While she looked, I did a little math in my head.

"Wouldn't they already be crushed?" After twenty-eight days the concrete would have completely cured, and the cylinders crushed with one of the large machines against the wall to test for comprehensive strength.

"We *always* save at least two." She started searching back at the beginning. "In the event there is litigation concerning one of our projects, we are required to do another test in front of an impartial engineer.

"Can you access the records from the original test?" I was hoping that would provide some insight.

She went to a table by the entry door where several computers were lined up. I leaned closer to her than I would have dared before seeing some sign of human emotion a few minutes ago. I watched her as she entered the job, location, and date of the sample. No results appeared in the search field. My phone vibrated while she worked and I snuck a peak at the screen. It was a smiley emoji.

"This is bad."

"Who would have had access to the samples? It appears they were taken before the cylinders were tested."

"There's not much for security here. People are in and out all day."

"Cameras?" I asked, looking around.

"No."

I guessed there was a traffic camera nearby that might show Brockmore's vehicle here, but scanning twenty-odd days of footage for evidence that would be circumstantial at best was too time-consuming to be worth it. Miami-Dade might have people for that, but I didn't. The theft could have occurred any time from the date of the pour, when the samples were brought in, to the date they were due to be tested—almost a month later.

I already knew he had done it. Though there was plenty of evidence leading to Brockmore, I finally had a motive. Knowing the concrete was subpar, Brockmore had removed the cylinders before they could be tested. Brockmore could easily ascertain that Larry Shelton was the inspector on the day the concrete was delivered from the job log. He would have done the testing as well and found them missing. He was killed before he could report it. I had a motive and a timeline now. "Would anyone know if several tests weren't done?"

"You could probably figure it out, but you'd have to look at the site logs and see what days they poured, then go back to the plant and check their records. The tests are just documentation after the fact."

Roslyn was still working the computer, trying to find something that wasn't there. I let her go and called Grace.

"Brockmore's our man," I started, and explained about the underwater explosion and the evidence Justine had found.

"That doesn't tie him to the murder," she said.

"I just need a little time," I said. Blowing the bridge at the exact moment when Shelton was driving underneath it was a tricky bit of business and a loose end that I would have to tie up, but I felt like I had enough for an arrest now and maybe a conviction if I could tie the missing cylinders to Brockmore.

"If he's not a flight risk, it's not worth bringing him in on a misdemeanor. Guy like that, owning a business and all, will be out on bail by midnight."

I disconnected and thanked Roslyn, who only nodded as she continued to try and find anything that would save her company. I heard her fingers slamming the keys as she became more anxious, and she barely acknowledged me when I left.

I sat in my truck. I had nowhere to go until Susan was able to update me with Brockmore's whereabouts. Sitting there I tried to think about the best way to reach her without alerting Brockmore, but the heat was making it hard to think. This could easily be the hottest day I had experienced here. It was somewhat akin to wrapping yourself in tin foil, basting in oil, and sitting in the sun. Even with the air conditioning on and the windows open, the late afternoon sun was countering the effect of either. A cluster of shade trees looked inviting and I moved the truck there. I wiped my brow waiting for the heat to dissipate and looked at my phone.

I had to do something and started typing in a message for Susan. Calling her would be better, but if she was with Brockmore, it might alert him. The last item in our text string hit me in the face. It was the emoji I had seen inside. I'd had thought it was from Allie and figured I would answer her later. Instead it was Susan's message. The smiley face must have meant that she had found him.

If I knew Susan and she had Brockmore occupied, they probably weren't at his office. As I turned out of the lot and started in the direction of the concrete plant, I realized my mistake. In my revenge-fueled rush to search the *Mud Man*, I should have included Brockmore's home and office in the warrant as well. Now, if I wanted to find any evidence I would have to deal with Martinez and whoever the judge on call for the weekend was, or do it illegally. I decided to have a look around the plant and decide.

It would have been helpful to know where Susan and Brockmore were. Martinez again was the easiest solution, but taking him away from his Friday evening happy hour, especially after his high-profile week, could go badly for me. Contacting Susan could compromise her. There was one option left: to track her.

It was a shot in the dark, especially for someone like Susan, who was both tech savvy and devious. It was no surprise that she hadn't shared her location with me. Frustrated and angry at myself for getting in a position where I had to rely on Susan McLeash, I texted Justine to see if she wanted to get a bite to eat. The pieces were all falling into place and I had the feeling this was going to be resolved soon—maybe tonight. I might as well get some fuel in me before it did.

I was still on the phone with Justine when I saw the door open and Roslyn appear. Her usually determined face was screwed up tight and even from here I could see the anger in her eyes.

"You still there?" Justine asked.

I paused, then started giving her a play by play as Roslyn went to her car and pulled out of the lot. Her tires screeched when they hit the asphalt. "I'm going to follow her."

"Let's not make any rash moves, Special Agent."

"I'll keep you posted—promise." I disconnected and went after her. Unless you were in the older neighborhoods near the coast, following someone in Miami was not all that hard. The surface streets run in a grid and are more like multi-lane highways with traffic lights than streets.

I slowed when I saw the yellow light on SW 252nd Street, but she had no intention of stopping. Swinging into the left lane, she made the light. I was still several cars behind and followed, expecting Martinez was going to get a picture from the red light camera on SW 176th Ave. She entered the Turnpike heading north.

I followed. The small light bar on the plain white park service truck gave me a little worry, but I guessed from the look on Roslyn's face when she left the testing plant that being followed wasn't on her radar—she was looking ahead. Using the larger SUVs and trucks for cover, I worked my way to within a hundred yards and stayed in the middle lane. Sitting on the bottom of the peninsula and heading north, she had the entire country open to her, but when she moved to the right hand lane just ahead of the exit to Highway 41, I had an idea where she was headed.

If she was going where I thought, the cylinders would likely be there. Without looking away, I slowed and reached for my phone. Justine's number was at the top of the call log, and I pressed the button to connect. "I think she's going to Brockmore Concrete," I said when she answered. "Might be good if you could get over there. I'm guessing he has the cylinders there."

"Why me? You should be calling Grace."

"If he has them, I want them taken into evidence the right way. He's moving up the line from defacing public property to breaking and entering if he stole them. It's time to nab him. They've got a regular mining operation there." I recalled the nuclear lake and heavy equipment. "Might be some evidence of the demolitions around, too, and we can get him for the murder of Larry Shelton and five others."

"Okay, I'm on my way, but call for backup, too."

I waited until Roslyn pulled off the highway and turned left on 41 before calling Grace. The call went to voicemail and I left her the details, then called the general dispatch number. After a runaround and getting kicked upstairs, I was promised backup. I set the phone down and focused on Roslyn's car. Turning left on Krome about a quarter mile after her, I stayed well back now that the traffic was lighter. There was no question now of where she was headed; Brockmore's plant was only a few miles away.

The lack of cover started to bother me. From a mile away, I could see the reflection of the sun off several windshields in the parking lot. When I was within a half-mile, I saw the twin to my truck sitting next to a tricked out late-model pickup.

It was too late to be proactive and I wouldn't know what was going on until I got there. It turned out I didn't have to worry about setting a trap. It looked like Susan was making a grab for glory and Roslyn meant to change it. From a quarter mile out, I saw Roslyn turn into the parking lot. A flatbed truck came up on my right, obstructing my view, but I knew it would do the same to her. Matching its speed, I moved closer, finally backing off just before the entrance to the plant.

Roslyn had reached the entrance. When I saw what I thought was a gun in her hand, I forgot about stealth and swerved to the right, entering the parking lot in a blur of gravel. Florida has a Castle Doctrine, which gives a person immunity from dealing with a deadly threat if they are in a legally occupied property. I expected a business qualified. I wasn't sure if Albert had a weapon, but I knew Susan did, and she wasn't afraid to use it.

Chapter 27

Roslyn was already inside and I hadn't heard a gunshot—yet—so I swung the pickup around the side of the building out of sight of the front entrance. If no one had been shot and they hadn't seen me, there was no point in broadcasting my presence. Exiting the truck, I removed my gun belt from the glove compartment and started toward a window that I thought was from Albert's office.

I buckled the belt around my waist, removed my weapon and checked the magazine and chamber. Keeping it in hand, I slid my back across the hot cinderblock wall until I could just see inside. It might have been the correct window, but all I saw was my own reflection in the heavy tint installed to keep the tropical sun at bay.

Just in case it was one-way, I ducked underneath it. I was heading toward the back corner of the building when I saw a glint of chrome from the parking lot. Changing direction, I ran to the front entrance and my heart dropped when I saw it was Justine.

I had called her in to help with the evidence, not to be a part of a gunfight. The last takedown we'd been through together hadn't ended well for her. I signaled for her to bring her car around the side by my truck and ran over.

"They're all inside. Roslyn, Albert, and Susan. At least two are armed." I didn't have to tell her that one of the two with a weapon was Susan. Justine had been a party to Susan's actions as well.

"We should wait for backup. You did call it in?" she asked. "What's the she-wolf all hell bent about?"

I checked my watch. "They should be here any minute." I thought about Roslyn. "She needs those missing cylinders to protect her company. Without them, they could be deemed complicit in this. With them, she can prove that it was the flawed concrete from Brockmore's plant."

We agreed that unless something drastic happened we would wait. Justine slid down behind her car, resting her back against the wheel. I sat down next to her, using the shade of the car both to keep us out of sight and block the sun. There were few cloudless afternoons in the summer here and I was witnessing firsthand how hot the sun could get.

Even in the shade, sweat dripped into my eyes. I removed my sunglasses and wiped my brow, wondering how much longer it was going to take for backup to arrive and what we were going to do once they got here. There was no cause to breach the building and I was thinking about texting Susan to see if I could get an update when I heard the back door open.

We couldn't see the back of the building from where we sat. I motioned for Justine to stay behind me and with my pistol extended before me I started to make my way to the corner of the structure. Suddenly a piece of heavy equipment fired up and I heard a gunshot ring off steel. Moving faster, I reached the back and peered around the corner.

Roslyn was in a firing stance near the back door, shooting at the back of a large loader moving away from her. She fired several shots then took off at a run after the machine. Heavy equipment can move quickly on a smooth surface, but as soon as it hits uneven ground, a runner can easily keep up. Roslyn was a runner and was slowly closing the gap.

Another shot rang out and we couldn't wait for backup any longer. They were at least a quarter mile away now, just by the northern end of the lake.

"Let's take the truck." I turned back to Justine. We both ran to the pickup. I handed my weapon to Justine and fumbled with the keys. Finally, the key slid into the ignition and after starting the engine, I pulled back in reverse and slammed the shifter into low gear. Whoever had made the decision to buy two-wheel drive government trucks, thinking Florida was flat, hadn't taken into account the amount of dirt and gravel roads we faced—or the potholes and ruts created by the rains.

But even without four-wheel drive, the truck easily caught up, and I saw a small metal building on the edge of the lake. It looked like that was their destination and I sped forward, taking a side road to cut them off. The loader reached it before Roslyn or I did, and I watched as Albert jumped down from the driver's seat and ran to the door.

I cursed when I saw Susan on the far side of the loader and again when I saw her weapon was drawn and she was facing Roslyn. The women were in firing stances, facing each other from fifty yards—a standoff. Briefly I hoped they would shoot each other. That thought left my mind as soon as Albert unlocked the steel door and swung it open.

Justine and I were off to the side and with Albert

focused on getting in the building and Susan and Roslyn on each other, we hadn't been seen. I used that to my advantage and after taking my weapon from Justine, left our truck and headed for the back of the building. Whatever was causing the standoff was inside—and I had a pretty good idea what it was.

When I got to the structure I could hear things being knocked aside as if Albert were searching for something inside. Then it was quiet for a second, and I moved around the far side of the building and saw him emerge. The two stainless steel cylinders he carried caught the sun as he ran toward the lake.

"Susan, stop him. That's evidence," I called, but she was focused on Roslyn, thinking she was protecting him. Just as she turned toward Albert I saw movement behind Roslyn. A quick look behind me confirmed Justine was gone.

NO formed on my lips, but I held back the word, not wanting to alert Roslyn. She remained with her gun pointed at Susan and I hoped her tunnel vision would work in our favor as Justine crept up behind her. I watched as she lowered herself like a cat into a crouch, preparing to spring forward. I said a silent prayer as I watched Justine launch herself across the five feet separating the two women.

She landed on Roslyn's back and immediately grabbed for her gun hand as the two women went to the ground. It might have been a fair fight had they been facing each other, but Justine had the element of surprise and quickly disarmed Roslyn, pulled her arm behind her back, and lifted her to her feet. I could see the triumphant look on her face as she marched her toward the truck.

A splash turned my attention back to Albert and Susan. He had used the fracas to ditch the cylinders in the lake. Susan stood motionless as if she didn't know what to do, but suddenly turned to him with her weapon raised.

This was where she was the most dangerous; the intersection of her emotions and the part of the brain that restrains you from doing something stupid.

"Susan. I have him covered. Lower your—"

She fired before I could get the last word out and I held my breath for a second. Albert dropped to his knees, but I realized when he put his hands behind his head that he hadn't been shot. Susan walked up behind him and I was just about to call out again when I heard sirens coming toward us.

The Miami-Dade cruisers came bouncing along the uneven road and reached us a few seconds later. While they took Roslyn and Albert into custody, I walked over to where Susan was standing.

"You have no evidence anymore. No one in their right mind will go into that water," Albert spat at me as he was marched to one of the cruisers.

"You okay?" I asked Susan.

"Probably shouldn't have fired."

Every dog needed a bone now and then and I offered one. "I'll say you were shooting back at Roslyn in self-defense. You'll get credit for the arrest as well."

She smiled and I knew I had done the right thing. Justine came up beside me and asked what I had said and agreed.

"You're not going to change her, and you're pretty much stuck with her. Maybe this'll buy some goodwill."

"What about the cylinders? We need that evidence to convict him."

"Nobody's diving in that muck, but I've seen you work a backhoe."

I looked around at the equipment nearby and saw an excavator. "You think you could have a quick look around the office before this place is overrun?" I expected with Miami-Dade here, word would get out and with the high profile of the case, that anyone, either on or off duty, within miles would be here soon. "Anything that might show how Brockmore timed the killing." That was the missing link in charging him with first-degree murder.

"We never got a warrant for his offices," Justine pointed out.

"I'd say shots fired is a good enough excuse."

She headed toward the office and I walked to the excavator.

The keys were in it and a few minutes later I had several scoops of green-tinged mud on the bank. The digging was easy, but had yielded no results. Looking at the growing pile of muck, I wondered if the consistency were similar to quicksand and the weight of the cylinders had taken them deep into the pit.

I relocated several feet away in order to spread the excavations out. The growing pile would only entrap the evidence. Scoop after scoop came out of the pit and I started getting frustrated. I took a break to look around and noticed that the site was indeed swarming with police, both in and out of uniform. With this many people in on it, it would no longer be a secret and I expected the media any second. Turning back to the controls, I started to lower the bucket when I noticed Justine coming from the office. From the look on her face, I could tell she had been more successful than I was.

"GPS got him!" she called out.

I stopped digging and turned to her.

"All the company vehicles have trackers—his truck included. I guess it's to keep track of employees and to write off the miles. When I checked his truck, he was within a quarter mile of the bridge when it collapsed." She grinned again.

I thought it might be enough, but we still needed the cylinders and I turned my attention back to the pit. Digging with renewed energy, I placed scoop after scoop on the bank with still nothing to show for it. I paused for a second, thinking, and studied the bright green water, wondering what I was missing.

Looking down at the machine, I saw what looked like a water line a few feet out of the water. It appeared I had misjudged the contours of the excavation and been too tentative. Now, assured by the mark that I was not going to sink, I eased the machine into the lake. Glancing around I saw I had an audience, probably betting when the lake would swallow me and rid the Miami-Dade police of my presence. Ignoring them, I continued forward until the water lapped against the top of the treads just inches away from the mark.

I started digging again, but I was far enough into the lake that I had to retreat several feet before I could deposit the muck onto solid ground. It was starting to get dark now and I guessed I had less than a half-hour before we would either need to postpone or bring in lights. Taking what I thought would be the last scoop, I moved the machine back to solid ground, swung the bucket to the side, and dumped its contents. As the muck slumped off, I could see the last of the sun reveal the stainless steel cylinders.

Chapter 28

We were anchored in twelve feet of water, just inside and to the north of the new reef site. I had entered the numbers of several of the sites we had scouted into the chart plotter and a blue icon displayed our location. While Allie prepared to roll over the gunwale I glanced over at the site of the new reef.

With the mooring buoys long gone and the coordinates not yet released to the public, the water above the site was empty. Besides the short amount of time the reef would have had to attract marine life, it was in the Lobster Sanctuary and off-limits to what I guessed to be a hundred boats dotting the horizon.

Allie was first in the water. Justine and I looked, bleary-eyed, over the side and followed her in. The embrace of the water woke me, and I floated down to join my daughter, watching her as she worked her way around the large coral heads.

Martinez had never changed my assignment, so I figured I deserved a little easy overtime. Between catching Brockmore and the new reef in the park this had been a banner week for him. Even Susan had gotten some love.

Allie frantically waved her tickle stick in my direction and I finned over to her. Before helping her, I looked over to where Justine was and saw a large burst of bubbles from an adjacent coral head. She must have found some herself.

Turning back to Allie, I released air from my BC and slowly lowered myself to the sand to get a better look at what Allie was so excited about. When the silt settled, I could see at least a dozen antenna protruding from a small ledge. Some of these openings ran deep into the coral structure, allowing the lobster easy refuge. If this one was shallow, we would have our limit on one dive.

The mesh bag attached to my BC hung up on a chunk of coral when I tried to unclip it, causing another minute to pass before the silt settled. When it did, the lobsters were still there. I nodded to Allie that I was ready and watched as she slowly reached the two-foot long rod in behind the lobster. With their strength in their tails, Lobsters swim backward. They needed a little nudge to make them feel like their backs were up against a wall, causing them to walk forward.

It was not as easy as it sounded, especially for two novices. The crustacean's instincts would have it kick backward. The tickle stick had to be perfectly deployed for each one to walk forward into the waiting net in Allie's hand. The first lobster reacted to the stick and there was a commotion below the ledge. It appeared we were lucky. If the ledge had led to a deep hole, they would be gone. Instead, when the sand settled, the antennas shyly started to feel the water outside the ledge.

I motioned for Allie to wait until they got comfortable and now, with a little experience, she was able to coax one out. Just as its tail became exposed she slid the net over it and looked over at me with a huge smile. We were only halfway there, and she had done her part. Now it was my turn. Reaching my gloved hand over the net, I grabbed the panicked lobster by the body, surprised at its strength when it tried to escape, and worked the net into the bag. Once inside, I released my hand and helped the lobster untangle itself from the net. It kicked down and I was able to retrieve the net and close the hoops that held the bag shut.

Our celebration was short-lived. Now that she had some experience, Allie was back at the ledge ready for more. One at a time, we picked off eight of what I guessed were a dozen. Several were too small and had to be released, but we left the ledge with six.

Justine was about fifty feet away, working another area. We swam over to her and I could see the bugs already in her bag. While she dug the last lobster out, I checked my air gauge, surprised to see that it had sunk below 500 psi. Despite being in only a dozen feet of water, I had almost exhausted my supply. I caught Allie's gauge suspended in the water and saw she had about the same. Justine would probably have more, but we had decided to stay a group. Once she had bagged the last lobster, we ascended to the surface.

"That was so cool!" Allie had dumped the lobsters onto the deck and was putting them in the cooler.

"Looks like twelve. Almost there," Justine said.

There is some instinct in us that makes it hard to stop the hunt, and I wanted to teach my daughter to resist it and learn to become a good steward of the environment and our resources.

"We've got some good spots left. How about we save some for tomorrow and check out the new reef?"

"Okay," Allie said.

I could tell she was disappointed, but hoped the bad dad attitude would be short-lived. After we had secured our catch and stowed the gear, Justine drove forward and I pulled the anchor. We changed places at the helm. I pressed down the throttle and spun the wheel in the direction of the new reef.

Looking to the north and east I could see the line of boats sitting just outside of the park boundaries. Marine biologists had studied the area and said that the sanctuary had been extremely effective in repopulating the park's reefs. Not knowing exactly where the imaginary line was, the divers beyond the boundary hoped the bounty, would wander onto the adjacent reefs and into their nets.

I zoomed in on the icon on the chart plotter that marked the reef, and slowed once I was close. Justine was already on the bow with the anchor in hand when I idled into the light breeze. When the boat was directly over the mark, I told her to throw the hook. With all the debris below, anchoring was easy and I expected one of us would have to do an additional drop to retrieve the hook before we left. After paying out about a hundred feet of line, Justine tied off the rode and we started to gear up.

I checked my watch and helped Allie onto the gunwale. She and Justine bailed backward into the water, surfaced, and gave the okay sign. We were in open water now, and diving to sixty feet we needed to be more organized. Having agreed to meet on the anchor line and descend together, they disappeared beneath the bow of the boat.

I took a deep breath, picked up my phone and sent a quick text. Hitting send, I geared up and was quickly in the water. There was little current and I met Justine and Allie at the anchor line. We all nodded and descended together, using the line to guide us to the reef.

Three days after we had set the first ball, the

debris was already coated in green and small fish swam in and out of the openings. Because the bridge portions had already been rubble, the explosions had done little noticeable damage except for maybe collapsing a few of the larger openings. We swam around the perimeter, surprised to see a Goliath grouper had already taken residence. I expected in another week the reef would be teeming with life.

I checked my watch and air, waiting in quiet anticipation for the sound of a boat that should be here any minute. As if on cue, ten minutes later I heard the sound of the engines approach and then stop. An anchor dropped into the sand outside the debris line and I looked over at Justine and Allie. We were forty-five minutes into our dive and it was time to surface.

Slowly, careful to ascend slower than our bubbles, we started toward the surface. I took the lead but a minute later caught a look from Justine. She pointed at the other hull just visible on the surface, indicating that I was going to the wrong boat. I ignored her and kicked hard in the direction of the larger boat, careful to stay at the same depth.

I could hear both Justine and Allie banging brass clips against their tanks to get my attention, but I continued toward the surface, hoping I would reach my destination before they could reach me.

Just five feet below the dive ladder, I stopped and waited. Justine looked angry and Allie scared as I kicked once toward the surface, hoping those looks would change.

We broke the surface together and I turned to them. Their looks had turned curious now. I swam between them, grabbed their hands, and swam backward a few feet so we could see the deck of the Interceptor.

"Get the hell out!" Justine yelled.

Allie looked confused.

On deck, Johnny Wells and crew were in their dress uniforms and Mariposa and her husband were off to the side.

"You good?" I asked Justine, then thinking I ought to say the words, asked her if she would marry me.

"You betcha," she said.

Get the next book in the Kurt Hunter Mystery Series

There is one word that brings out the worst in people: TREASURE.

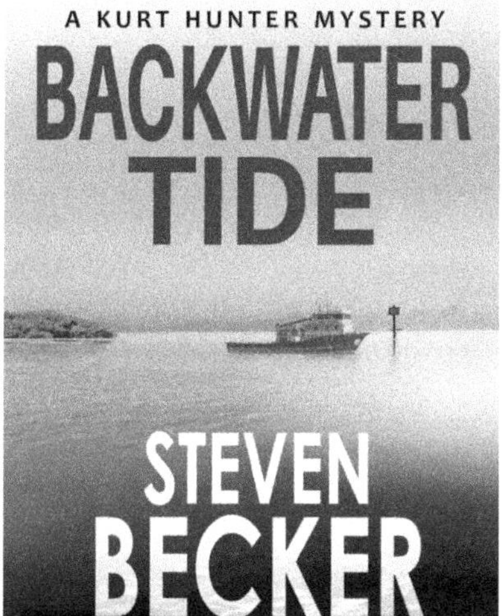

When special agent Kurt Hunter finds a boat adrift in the Biscayne National Park with the dead body of a famous treasure hunter aboard, the race is on to find his killer. Alliances shift and the bodies start to pile up as Kurt and Justine navigate the devious and dangerous world of treasure hunters to find the killer.

From the iconic Intracoastal Waterway of Miami to the beauty of the Biscayne National Park, this new mystery from bestselling author, Steven Becker, reveals the good, the bad, and the ugly of South Florida.

Get it now!

About the Author

Always looking for a new location or adventure to write about, Steven Becker can usually be found on or near the water. He splits his time between Tampa and the Florida Keys - paddling, sailing, diving, fishing or exploring.

Find out more by visiting

www.stevenbeckerauthor.com

or contact me directly at

booksbybecker@gmail.com

Get my starter library First Bite for Free when you sign up for my newsletter

http://eepurl.com/-obDj

First Bite contains the first book in each of Steven Becker's series:

- **Wood's Reef**
- **Pirate**
- **Bonefish Blues**

By joining you will receive one or two emails a month about what I'm doing and special offers.

Your contact information and privacy are important to me. I will not spam or share your email with anyone.

Wood's Reef

"A riveting tale of intrigue and terrorism, Key West characters in their full glory! Fast paced and continually changing direction Mr Becker has me hooked on his skillful and adventurous tales from the Conch Republic!"

Pirate

"A gripping tale of pirate adventure off the coast of 19th Century Florida!"

Bonefish Blues

"I just couldn't put this book down. A great plot filled with action. Steven Becker brings each character to life, allowing the reader to become immersed in the plot."

Get them now (http://eepurl.com/-obDj)

Also By Steven Becker

Kurt Hunter Mysteries

Backwater Bay

Backwater Channel

Backwater Cove

Backwater Key

Backwater Pass

Backwater Tide (Sept 2018)

Mac Travis Adventures

Wood's Relic

Wood's Reef

Wood's Wall

Wood's Wreck

Wood's Harbor

Wood's Reach

Wood's Revenge

Wood's Betrayal

Tides of Fortune

Pirate

The Wreck of the Ten Sail

Haitian Gold

Will Service Adventure Thrillers

Bonefish Blues

Tuna Tango

Dorado Duet

Storm Series

Storm Rising

Storm Force

CPSIA information can be obtained
at www.ICGtesting.com
Printed in the USA
BVHW072233110319
542319BV00003B/284/P

9 781732 596009